THE
GARAGE
GUERRILLA

COLLIN PEARCE

For the Family

Introduction

The 1960s can most simply be described as an interesting time. It was a decade that changed society and reshaped the world, but for a small population of unstable Americans, this period potentially defined them. Something within them took hold and allowed them to become what they ultimately would. Were they a product of their twisted minds and time, or merely a statistical outlier bound to appear in any population? That, we might never understand. But what is clear is that the timeframe between the late 60s to the early 80s produced more serial killers in the United States than the nation has ever seen.

Many claim to know what makes a serial killer. They surmise that the right combination of factors exposed to any individual during their childhood can spawn a future filled with murder. As if the urge to kill comes from a virus that only festers in the right circumstances. This is as good an understanding of these people as any other guess. It isn't hard to believe that a person exposed to a harsh childhood might choose to live a harsh life. That thought finds a way to put meaning into something that, before, appeared utterly meaningless.

The reality is that the human condition is fascinating because we can only experience it as ourselves. We can watch and communicate with one another, but the ambitions and thoughts of those around us will always remain unknown. So, as for the late 60s to the early 80s, you can call it "situational opportunity" or "psychopathic congruity," but either way, the only thing we will ever truly understand is that for some reason, seemingly ordinary people decided to make monsters of themselves.

Chapter 1

Riverwood, Colorado, was known for its nice neighborhoods just west of Denver. Recently incorporated as a city in January of 1969, the area had a new feeling to its older roots that went back to the 1800s. It's westerly reaching developments were spread out between small farms and ranches that sat just on the edge of the front range. Most of the homes were built in the time after the Second World War, designed in classic track home fashion. The type where the same house sat two or three lots down and were only distinguishable by a different paint color.

The trees dated the neighborhoods to the time they were built. Twenty-year-old aspens, pines, and maples stood in lawns down most streets, but it was the giant cottonwoods that gave the area its ever-autumn feel. They would sway in the wind, creak and croak, dropping hand-size leaves that seemed to litter gutters and forgotten yards almost all year long. The cottonwoods twisted behind houses, following an old ditch trail that meandered its way through Riverwood's neighborhoods, creating small backways and narrow parks for kids to play or a place to walk the dog.

Sitting a hair outside of Denver, crime wasn't a common occurrence in the suburbs. The cry of a coyote or a lonely dog was more common at night than sirens. Just beyond the neighborhood stood the gates to the Rockies beckoning travelers, adventurers, and campers into the mountains. Purple peaks perched west with snow-white caps, evergreens and the occasional blinding reflection from the aluminum campers that crawled the mountains in the day.

This was where Abigail Thompson had purchased a home, in a neighborhood she loved. Her house fell under the new city limits of Riverwood and she had lived in it for the past five years. 1969 had just begun but the days were already starting to seem longer. Although the new year buzz of business was keeping her later than usual, Abby was still predictably home from work around the same time. She always shopped at the same place and made it home to turn on the same lights that illuminated her routine life. Her habits followed something that most working people can relate to.

As a divorced woman in her 40s with her only son

living on his own, her daily routine and her job had become the most reliable part of her life. In her piece of Riverwood, she blended into the crowd with the other passersby. She would often wear a big smile and could keep a warm conversation if one ever arose, but for the most part, she kept to herself.

She spent a lot of her time with a woman she worked with, Susan Collins. The two carpooled to work together. They both held the same job at a nearby car dealership and three years ago had decided to share the ride. This week, it happened to be Susan's turn to drive.

It was the first Wednesday in the month of February and approximately a quarter after 7:00 p.m. when Susan's brown 1966 Ford Country Sedan pulled to a stop in front of Abby's house at 1722 Shoshone. Engine exhaust barreled into the gutter and slowly flowed over the lawn. Abby stepped out of the car and turned to say good night to Susan before she drove away down the street.

It was dark and the dim glow from the neighborhood streetlights cast a color in their wake that could only be described as melancholy. Abby's house fell behind the shadows and sat in a dull, quiet lot. It looked colder near her home. Its frosted over yard and lightless windows didn't appear welcoming.

Abby looked toward the house with dinner on her mind and started up her driveway. Once inside, she stepped into an unlit entry and fumbled for the lights.

Her visible breath let her know that her house was just slightly warmer than the frigid night on the other side of the door. As cold as she kept it, one could have mistaken it for an abandoned home. Relying on just one income, she tried her best to live marginally. The fact that she had gone through the darkest days of winter and hadn't broken a pipe was a miracle.

She made her way to the kitchen and turned on the light. Dinner would be a can of chili again. She took a clean pot from her drying rack and placed it on the stovetop. She found a lone can of chili in her cupboard and spooned it into the pot. Abby tried to throw the empty can into the trash under her sink but found it full. She sighed, remembering that Thursday morning was trash day. She had a lazy habit of forcing whatever she could into the trash bin in her kitchen until she was forced to take it out to the garage.

Annoyed, she decided to take care of it before the night turned too cold. She grabbed the garbage can out from under the sink and began to slide it towards the garage door near the back of the kitchen. Using one hand to open the door the weight of the trash can held her back, but with a grunt and a wince she lifted it down onto a step leading into the garage. The door began to close behind her as the trash can pulled her along. She didn't have time to reach for the lights before the door shut, leaving her in darkness.

Abby shuffled the trash can down another step. She reached her hand out to find the light somewhere on the wall. Cold, and blind in the dark, she tried her best to remember where the switch was. She slid her hand around on the wall and began to think she'd never find it when a sound made the hairs on the back of her neck stand.

She froze, hand still on the wall, and promptly forgot about the light. She kept her eyes towards the wall, hoping that they would adjust to the dark, and listened closely for the noise to come back. It had sounded like a shoe softly stepping over glass on her garage floor. The noise was too pronounced for her to dismiss and her imagination began to fill the gaps her eyes couldn't see.

She turned and looked out into the blackness, but nothing came into focus. Silence blanketed the room. Another step came, slightly heavier than the last. Abby quickly came to the terrifying realization that there may be another person in her garage. Her mind began to race. Was this person here to steal her car? She had kept her breathing low to listen better, but now she couldn't keep it from quickening. She thought to herself that maybe if she yelled out to this person they'd leave. If she could get the lights on, if she could see whoever it was, they'd have to run. She continued searching on the wall for the light switch as she tried to reason out the sound of someone else moving through her garage.

To her relief, her hand found the switch and she pushed it as fast as she could. It snapped up, making a loud *thud* that echoed in the garage. The darkness remained. The light hadn't worked.

Abby panicked and quickly tried the light two more times. It echoed again but still left her in the dark. Her fear deepened as she turned back for the door. She threw her hand on the knob and was about to twist it over when the sound of metal sliding over her car paralyzed her.

She couldn't bring herself to look toward the source of the sound. A visceral feeling of horror occupied every part of her body. She wanted to cry out but the only sound she could make came as a groan through her gasping throat. She desperately wished she had the ability to scream, to yell at this person and get through the door, but her body had overwritten her brain.

Abby was left standing on the last step to her house, shaking in fear. Her heart was beating through her chest. She caught up with herself and snapped her head around towards the noise. Her eyes darted across the garage and finally adjusted to the dark. They fell upon a silhouetted figure of a man on the other side of her car. The figure lifted something in its right hand and pointed it at her. She turned back for the door and twisted the handle, but never made it inside.

Four shots echoed down Shoshone Street, sparking a chain reaction of barking dogs and bedroom lights. A silhouette emerged from the side garage door of Abigail Thompson's house and quickly crept down the driveway, running past the dim streetlights and avoiding the prying eyes of curious neighbors.

~ ~ ~

Just under an hour after the gunshots startled the neighborhood, detectives Sean Kennedy and David Maxwell stepped onto the sidewalk in front of 1722 Shoshone. They had been working together in the area for the last four years as part of the Denver PD but were recently incorporated into the Riverwood station once the new city was established. Most of the homicides they responded to this far west of Denver tended to be dumped bodies, left in shallow graves and found in remote fields. The detectives were accustomed to following dogs around the hills, hoping to sniff out mistakes from Denver's crime families and cleaning up after poorly planned murders. An actual homicide in the subdivisions was rare but got a lot of attention when it happened.

"Detectives, welcome to the show," said Bill Hawthorne, a chubby older patrolman who had been one of the first to respond to the crime scene and who had radioed in the homicide.

Hawthorne was now directing foot traffic outside in the dark and keeping curious neighbors back. He greeted the detectives briefly before moving on to meet more onlookers.

Sean and Dave moved past him and made their way up the driveway to the front door. As they stepped into the house the detectives immediately ran into the county forensics team scattered between the kitchen and the garage.

Sean skipped the hellos and got right to it. "Hey guys, where's Christopher?"

One of the heads popped up to reply for the group. "He's in the garage with the body."

The detectives carefully made their way through the kitchen and stopped at the door to the garage. It was wide open. The garage was dark, but they could see a flashlight pointing around. Its light shined off a trail of blood that ran under a parked car. A woman's body was just underneath the steps of the open door.

Dave called out into the room. "Christopher, you in there?"

Christopher Williams was the County Forensics team lead and took on most, if not all, the area's homicides. His years of experience as a criminalist made him crucial to investigations. He yelled back to Dave from in the garage. "Yeah, come on in."

Dave stepped into the garage and kept his eyes down on the dead body in front of him. The woman had a gunshot in the side of her face and three in her back. He stepped around the body to let Sean in and couldn't help but curse under his breath. The site turned his stomach.

Blood covered the door and the wall around it. Sean stepped in and glanced over at Christopher, who was scribbling away in a notebook lit by his flashlight.

"Well, what do we know?" asked Sean.

Christopher put down his pen and turned to face the detectives. "She took four shots from a .45 caliber pistol. The side door has a glass pane busted out and the overhead light is missing."

Sean bent down and examined the bloody corpse. He had a camera with him and took photos. The bullet to her face had done a lot of damage where it exited.

Christopher walked over and handed Dave the woman's purse. "We found this inside. Her name is Abigail Thompson. She's forty-five years old and it appears she works at one of the car dealerships downtown."

Dave started to pace around the dark garage. He led his flashlight all over the room, from the side door to the ceiling. He soon pulled out a notebook as well and began to scratch in his own notes. He could see his breath as he said, "So, whoever did this obviously broke in through the back-garage door. And what are we thinking about this missing light? It might've been removed by our killer. Did you find any broken or discarded bulbs around?"

"No," Christopher shook his head as he replied. "The only glass came from the door."

Dave nodded and continued looking around the garage. "What about in the house?"

"As far as we can tell, nothing looks thrown around or out of place. All her jewelry is still in its box. It looks like nothing happened in the house."

Sean got up from kneeling near the body. "This feels personal. The house wasn't robbed. Her clothes are still on, and the car is in the garage." He looked over at Dave with a puzzled expression.

Dave shared his thoughts. This one wasn't giving them any clear motive right off the bat.

Christopher pointed to the other side of the car and said, "The shells rolled over there."

Sean walked over to where Christopher pointed and found four .45 caliber shells. He looked back at Christopher. "Think you can identify the gun?"

Christopher nodded but didn't speak.

Sean continued to look around, but there wasn't much to miss in the small garage.

He turned back over to Christopher and asked, "What about prints?"

"Didn't get anything on the broken door and nothing on the car where our gunman was standing. But we were able to get some off the car's driver-side handle and the door back into the house. We looked for footprints, too, but I couldn't see any outside. Ground's still too cold."

Sean nodded and sighed. He hoped they could learn more from witnesses. He gave Dave a head nod signaling he was ready to wrap it up. It wouldn't be long before the body would be taken to the coroner's office. After the autopsy, they'd learn more about Mrs. Thompson's final moments, but for the time being, they needed to hear what the neighbors had seen. The detectives took one last look in the garage before stepping back into the house.

Speaking to witnesses could always be a painstaking process but it was one of the most rewarding ones when it produced valuable information. The dispatcher had told them they had at least four calls about gunshots coming from 1722 Shoshone and maybe four more throughout the neighborhood regarding the commotion caused by the barking dogs. They knew that they would find plenty of people to talk to.

The detectives moved out in front of the house. Officer Hawthorne was standing in the same place he'd met them before at the bottom of the driveway.

Dave waved him over and asked, "Did you talk to any houses before you checked out this one?"

Hawthorne nodded. He pointed at the house next door to the garage. "Dispatch had me show up there. We spoke briefly and after that, I came over here to check it out. The house looked empty until I walked over near the side garage door."

Dave looked over at Sean. "We'll start with them."

The detectives left Hawthorne in front of the house and made their way over to the home next door. It was getting close to 9:00 p.m., but most of the houses still had their lights on. Police lights were dancing throughout the block, encouraging curiosity. At any moment, a gurney would emerge carrying a covered body off to the coroner's office.

It was an interesting night in the suburbs.

Sean walked up to the house first. He rang the doorbell and they patiently waited. Dave pulled out his notebook and looked over the information he had scribbled down in the garage.

A middle-aged man and woman came to the door.

"Good evening, folks," said Sean, "Sorry to disturb you. We're with the Riverwood Police Department." Sean started the conversation quickly. He wanted to get as much out of their time as possible. "We were hoping you could help us by answering a couple questions. Were you one of the houses that called?"

The man nodded and replied, "Yes sir."

"What time would you say that was at?"

"Around seven forty."

Dave wrote the number down. They needed to get a timeline together.

"Did you hear any yelling or any sort of an argument? Anything like that?"

"No. Just the gun shots. Is everything ok?" The man asked, practically squinting. "What happened?"

Sean sighed. He was used to giving people bad news.

"Unfortunately, your neighbor has passed away."

The man's wife covered her mouth. "Oh god."

Sean gave the couple a few seconds to take in the news before he asked his next question. "Did you see anything, by chance? Did you glance out of a window after you heard the gunshots?"

"No. I looked but I couldn't see anything."

Sean was upset to hear that. They needed a witness. The sooner they could get a description of who they were looking for, the better their odds were. As of now, the detectives still didn't know what they were dealing with.

Sean asked them one last question, "What about earlier in the evening? Anything interesting happen at your neighbor's house? Any cars you haven't seen before?"

The man tried to think about the question but shook his head. "Nothing I can think of."

Dave had barely taken any notes from the couple. He got their names and jotted down their address before Sean ended the conversation and thanked them for their time.

The detectives headed back down to the street. This time they decided to walk over to the house directly across from Abby's. Its residents had the best chance of seeing anything from their windows after the shooting. Sean took the lead again and rang the doorbell.

An old man opened the door in a night robe.

"Good evening, sir," said Sean. "We're with the

Riverwood Police. Would you mind answering a couple of questions for us?"

The old man folded his arms and leaned up against his door. "No. Not at all. In fact, I had called in earlier. Is everything ok?"

Dave had his notebook back out. This man could have seen something. Sean broke the bad news and then asked, "Could you tell us what time you called in?"

The man's face tightened. "Yeah. It was maybe a quarter to eight."

Dave started a new page for the conversation and took down the time.

Sean continued. "Did you hear anything odd before you heard the gunshots?"

"No. I was watching television. I only heard the shots."

"Were you able to see anything?"

"Yeah," The man nodded. "I came to the window and peeked through the blinds. I saw a guy running down the street."

Dave began scratching in his notebook. They needed to hear everything he could describe about the runner. Dave asked, "Could you make out what he looked like?"

The man peered out into the street as if he was trying to see the runner again. "It was very dark. But he looked young and thin. He was fast. I only saw him for a brief second."

Sean tried to squeeze out more. "Could you give us a general height, race or describe the clothing?"

The man thought about it and responded. "Average height. I couldn't make out his face or anything, but he was wearing long pants and a jacket. I'm sorry it was just too dark for me to say exactly."

The detectives were again disappointed. They were hoping for more, but it was a start. Sean asked the man a couple more questions before ending the conversation as Dave took the man's name and address and finished his notes. The two were used to having to piece together the night from different witnesses. It usually meant a long couple of hours after responding to a crime scene and having the same conversation over and over.

They walked back down to the street and looked for another house to try. The Coroner's truck had already moved the body out for autopsy. They still needed more before they could put out a helpful description on the radio and time was quickly passing.

Dave looked over to Sean and said, "The cruisers can't do much on looking for a young male."

"Another house might have what we need, or hopefully dispatch got another call."

Dave didn't respond but Sean could sense that he was already anxious. Dave hated the stress that followed a homicide and with no immediate leads, it looked like the detectives would have their work cut out for them.

Sean thought out loud. "This might be a case where we'll have to rely on the back work. See if any red flags come up when we notify next of kin and friends. If she's dating anyone or has an ex, he's our first look."

Dave nodded and pointed at the house next to the one they had just interviewed. He wasn't ready to start talking about their plans for the next day. "Let's hit a few more houses. Somebody else had to see something."

Chapter 2

It was mid-April of 2018, and Jake Caldwell got to the station early. For him, it was day one of the big time and he wanted to make sure he looked like he meant business. He had spent the last five years as a patrolman out of a smaller city nearby and had just accepted the job of detective in Riverwood.

Police Chief Mason Kelly watched him walk through the door and called out to him. "Jake, you're early."

Jake paused just after the entrance. "Morning, Sir. I wanted to make sure that I timed the commute right."

Kelly smiled. "Well, we're excited to have you onboard. Come on in."

Jake returned the smile and walked over towards the chief. Kelly turned his head and called out to someone sitting in a cubicle. "Hey Julie, come meet the new guy."

Julie Steiner had been the youngest detective in the Riverwood Crimes Against Persons division, or the "homicide unit," before Jake showed up. She was experienced for her age and had recently transferred over from another division. She walked over and looked at Jake.

He was young and seemed a little bit boy scout-ish. She politely greeted him and shook his hand. "How are you doing? Welcome to the fun."

She looked back over at Chief Kelly. "Is he going to be working with me?"

The chief nodded his head. "That's the plan. He'll shadow you once we think he's ready for the field. Would you mind showing Jake where we set him up?"

"Of course."

Julie gestured for Jake to follow and led him back towards the cubicles.

The station was old and musty. It looked more like an elementary school from the outside than a police station. The building was built with red brick and had large front windows. Its masonry had settled into itself over time and the old mortar between the bricks withered deep under each layer. It was positioned just in front of a cluster of businesses near a strip mall.

To the occasional shopper, the police station was easy to miss. It sat next door to a softly lit diner called the Ralston Cafe. Most of the Riverwood police force took to the diner for a break and a bite to eat. It had been there as long as the station and from the amount of police traffic inside, it could easily be mistaken as another part of it.

The restaurant had banned cigarettes, as had every other business in the state, but it still smelled like the smoking section wherever you sat. It was a classic place that usually served pancakes, potatoes and bacon or the 'works' if you're used to diner cooking. It gave the whole strip mall a greasy smell that clung to the air and hung around the station.

"Is this my spot?" asked Jake, as he looked over at a small cleared off desk in a dark cubicle.

"Yeah, that's where we got you situated," replied Julie. She pointed it out and then walked away to the break room.

Jake took a seat and dropped down his bag of notepads and pens. The desk was isolated and poorly lit by overhead fluorescent lighting. The big windows in the front of the building seemed to be the only ones apart from a small window in a back-exit door. Jake looked around his desk, excited. He was ready to start this new chapter in his life. Becoming a detective had always been his dream and even though it was in the quiet town of Riverwood, he couldn't have been prouder.

Julie came back around the corner from the break room with two cups of coffee and handed one to Jake.

"Here, you're going to need this. We call this cluster of cubicles 'the bullpen'. This will be your corner of it. I'm sure you remember your first day as a patrolman but however boring that was, this is worse, trust me."

Julie tried to take a little sip of her coffee, but it was still too hot for her to drink. She went on, "So, here's how today and unfortunately the next few weeks are going to go for you. They're going to pair you up with an old-timer. It's looking like it'll be Captain Spears. The District Attorney, Deborah Kettner, thought it'd be a good idea for new investigators joining the force to go over cold cases with a veteran. This is so the case gets reviewed with a new perspective and so the old-timer can coach you through the investigative process."

Julie blew on her coffee and took a sip. She pursed her lips and made a disgusted face. "Shit's bitter."

She kept the coffee in her hand and continued. "The DA's thought process here is that you'll get some training in how the department handles certain scenarios and in doing so, these old cold cases get another look. It's a win-win. The only issue is that the incoming current work doesn't stop, and I could already use your help."

Jake didn't know what to say. Getting thrown out into the field right away sounded like what he'd signed up for, but it was also a bit intimidating. Reviewing cold cases would be a snooze after being out on the streets for the past five years, but maybe it would help him to read up on what he was walking into.

He was curious about how much attention the cold cases received. He asked, "Are we the only ones looking into these old cases?"

Julie gave her head a non-committal shake. "Yes and no. Some cases get more eyes on them than others. The Sheriff's office and the Colorado Bureau of Investigations both get into cold cases, but the truth is there are a lot more cold cases out there than investigators looking at them. The DA wants as much overlap and attention given to these cases as possible due to their lack of success in being solved. It was one of the promises that got her elected."

Jake nodded. It made sense to him. He just wanted to know how long he would be reading old paperwork. Julie had mentioned weeks.

He asked, "How long does this last?"

"It's up to the senior officer that you'll be working with. I really can't say."

Jake finally took a sip of his coffee. If Julie was right, then he would need a lot of it. It sounded like he was about to do more reading than he'd done since college.

Julie drained what was left of her coffee and began to walk away. "I'll go let the chief know you're ready. After that, Spears should be by any minute."

Jake waved goodbye to Julie and tried to drink more of his coffee. He was impressed by how quickly Julie had drunk hers. It wasn't the type of coffee you put down for the taste. It was bitter and strong, the type of stuff that gave you a head rush just smelling it. He settled in his seat a little and began to mentally prepare himself for the cold cases coming his way.

It wasn't long before Jake looked up from his desk and watched an older guy come around the corner of the bullpen. The man looked clean, still stocky and had impeccably pressed clothes. He walked right up to Jake and stuck his hand out.

"You must be Jake. Glad to have you on. I'm Captain Alonzo Spears. You get a cup of coffee?"

Jake shook the man's hand and held up his cup. "Yeah, I did, thanks."

Spears looked excited to get started and said, "Chief Kelly wanted me to show you the ropes. I've been doing this for a long time and I'm hoping to be on the way out soon, so it seems fitting."

The captain took a seat on Jake's desk and continued. "The DA wants us to go over cold cases for the next couple of weeks so you can understand our order of operations before you're hit with the real deal backing up a lead detective. Did the chief fill you in?"

Jake politely shook his head. "No. Julie did."

Spears nodded and kept talking. "Being a detective is the natural next step in your career. You'll use the street smarts you gained over the last five years as a patrolman to uncover the motivations and methods behind the cases that you'll see. Through this exercise, you'll get a little taste of how that looks."

Spears paused. "It goes without saying that reviewing cold cases is a different psychology then taking on a live case. We also understand that a few weeks is an incredibly short time to dive into any case. Most require a lot of attention and that's why we leave an open door policy on all our cold cases. Once we turn you out into the field, you'll be encouraged to look back into any of the files we review as you see fit. By joining the Riverwood station you're inheriting a piece of our workload, past and present. So, don't be shy, you won't be stepping on any toes."

Spears took a sip of coffee and continued, "I won't be this lecturing the whole time. We'll go through the cases together and for most of them I'd like you to take the lead, so you get your juices flowing."

Jake liked the sound of that. He had worried that Spears would hold his hand for the next few weeks. He asked, "When do we start?"

The captain got off Jake's desk and looked towards the stairs near the back exit. "We start today. We keep most of the old files and any relevant evidence downstairs. Everything else is out in the warehouse."

Jake followed Spears back to a stairwell near the exit sign. As they made their way down the air turned stale. The building didn't have enough ventilation on the ground floor and what air did happen to seep into the basement smelled as if it had been there since the building was first erected. It was as if they had descended into a completely different atmosphere.

Spears flipped on a hallway light at the end of the stairs, showing the layout of the basement. There was a table against the wall and two doors opposite each other that read Case Room and Evidence.

Spears pulled out a set of keys and opened the Case Room. He flipped another switch and fluorescent lights struggled to life. The room illuminated, showing rows of labeled cabinets.

"In here is every cold case that we have. Every case going back to '69." Spears stepped into the room and continued, "When a case gets too old, we move most of its files and evidence to the warehouse but keep a general overview file of it here. This is so we can keep space for more recent cases and consolidate the older ones. The files are kept in chronological order."

Jake followed Spears into the room, looking down the rows of file cabinets as he moved.

Spears stopped and looked over at Jake, who was aimlessly walking about the room. "I know it looks like a lot for a quiet place, but 50 years of cold cases adds up."

Jake listened to Spears as he meandered around the cabinets. He couldn't help but wonder how many secrets they hid.

Spears called out to him. "See one you like?"

Jake looked back, confused. "How are we supposed to do this? Do you want me to just pick a year?"

"Yeah. We'll start that way. Pick a year, choose a file, open her up and we'll go from there."

Jake turned back around and walked up to a cabinet that read 1985. He opened it up and began thumbing through the files. His hand landed on one that he started to pull out, but he stopped as Spears interjected.

"Eh, eh, not that one. It's damn near the Da Vinci Code. I'd like to go through a couple of basics first."

Jake moved his hand over to a much smaller file and pulled it up. Spears made sure he grabbed the right-sized file and spoke as he headed out of the room. "That'll work for now. We're only going to focus on the overview of the case. Let's take it out to the table."

Jake closed the file cabinet and followed Spears back out of the room.

The two men sat down at the table outside of the Case Room. Jake dropped the file down and it made a surprisingly loud smack as it landed. Spears put his hand on the file, "Before we get into any of these old cases, I want to emphasize that they all lack the benefit of time, which is arguably the most crucial piece to an ongoing investigation. As you respond to a homicide, time is immediately against you. Leads come in, suspects and people of interest arise, but the longer it takes to make an arrest the greater the chances are that the offender you're after is clearing their tracks and changing their location."

Jake nodded as the captain continued. "These days, the average clearance rate across the country for homicides is close to sixty percent. Meaning that forty percent of the time, law enforcement can't make an arrest. That means we have a lot of new cases like the one in front of us."

Jake already knew that the statistics weren't on their side, but he was curious about what kind of benefit they could even give the old cases. He knew it was a learning exercise for him, but what more could they do that the original detectives hadn't already tried?

Spears answered his question before Jake could ask it. "Without time on our side and through the lens of hindsight, what we can offer these cases is mainly a renewed look into things like DNA or private and personal information that we now have access to on the internet. Trying to work with those tools paired with better synchronization between law enforcement agencies can open some new doors."

Jake raised his eyebrows. "DNA? How would we go about that?"

"When we review a case, sometimes we'll find DNA evidence left behind that hasn't been processed into the system. The best example for this would be a sexual assault. If the investigative team received a rape kit from the hospital after the incident, then we know for a fact that it contains the DNA from our offender. If we come across one of these cases, then we will move the rape kit to the crime lab so it can be processed into the system if it hasn't already been uploaded. However, there's a catch. They started doing rape kits in the late 70s and our system didn't come into place until the 2000s, so frustratingly enough we will find cases only involving a sexual assault that have timed out their statute of limitations but were never placed in the system. That, or the kit was flat out thrown away because it timed out."

Jake's eyes widened. "What's the statute of limitations on rape?"

Spears shook his head. "Twenty years. That's why in older cases we mainly look at homicides or a case involving both. There's no statute of limitations for a homicide."

Jake couldn't believe it. It didn't make sense to him, but he wanted to know more. He asked, "So if we find a case with testable DNA, what's this system we put it into?"

"It's called CODIS — the Combined DNA Index System — which is an ever-growing national database of DNA from missing persons, suspects, arrestees and convicted felons. It started in the late 90s but really came around in the 2000s."

"What happens if we find a case with testable DNA that doesn't match anything on CODIS?"

"Nothing," said Spears, flatly. "If we don't already have our offender's DNA then that's our last chance. If the man's not in the system, then we won't know who he is. All we can do is pray that eventually, he'll show up in the system. Which, in a lot of cases, means waiting for that offender to commit another crime and hopefully getting caught."

"Are kits the only sure way we can get DNA on a cold case?"

Spears shook his head again. "No. We can get DNA off anything as long as it still has some sort of bodily fluids on it. Clothes or other items where we find blood, saliva, skin or hair."

Jake took a deep breath and exhaled. It was a lot to think about. Spears shoved the file under his hand over to him and gestured at it. "Go ahead. Open her up, let's start this thing."

Jake grabbed the file and slid it closer. He put a finger under the manila folder and opened it up.

The file was titled, *Jackson Tilman Homicide May 8, 1985*. Jake skimmed the file until he found its summary:

Victim is a white male in his 30s. Found dead in his motel room in the Comfort Motel off Kipling Street by a cleaner. Cause of death appears to be one gunshot through the right side of his head. A possible suicide note was left on the dresser only reading, "Sorry," and signed with a big "J." No gun was found in the room but the casing to a .22 caliber bullet was found under the bed.

Jake flipped past the case overview and found a few pictures. The photos were graphic. He grunted as he thumbed through them. Spears smiled at his reaction, "Yep, you got to make sure you've had your first cup of joe before you start digging through this shit. Makes the stomach a little uneasy."

Jake continued through the pictures and went back to the forensics team's report. Spears was watching how Jake went about the file and talked to him as he turned the pages. "The first page is like a summary. That's the paperwork that the detectives put together. It will give you the lowdown on the case. After that, you'll have the forensics team's write up — that will be more detailed. And lastly, you'll have the coroner's report. That will give you your details on the victim, everything from eye color to blood alcohol percentage."

Jake continued to read until he took his eyes off the paperwork and looked up at the captain. He explained, "This case is of a lone male found with a suicide note and a bullet in his head. The detectives believed that it was a homicide staged to look like suicide. The kicker is that there's no gun. A man in a neighboring room claimed he heard footsteps after the gunshot. However, there were no witnesses. The victim was a truck driver based in Arkansas, but they couldn't identify any of his family or friends."

Spears listened and then asked Jake a question. "Did the coroner match the bullet hole to the casing?"

Jake looked back through the report and nodded his head. "Yeah. They did."

"Does it say anything else about the gun?"

"It says the coroner estimated the victim had died eight to twelve hours before he was found. The investigative team did note that there was enough time for someone to find the body and take the gun. The door was unlocked."

Spears mulled the situation over in his head. "Does the coroner's report show anything odd in his toxicology? Could have been a bad drug deal."

Jake scanned the report and shook his head. "No. He was a little drunk, but nothing else was in his system. The report doesn't list any drug paraphernalia found in the room, either."

"Was he robbed?"

"Doesn't say anything about that."

The captain had heard enough. There wasn't much for them to go on.

He asked, "What does the case have kept in evidence?"

Jake flipped to the back and found the evidence list and replied, "Looks like the suicide note and the .22 shell."

"So, we have a dead man found with no drugs, not robbed and next to a suicide note. Sounds like this is our first dud."

Jake slid the paperwork out to the middle of the table and asked, "A dud? What's that?"

Spears smiled. "Basically, a case that's just a royal pain in the ass. It's what we call a case with no leads, no witnesses and no hope."

He grabbed the file from the middle of the table and closed it. He looked back at Jake and said, "There's nothing we can do with this. Let's put it back and try another. I'll write down the case numbers on the ones we review so we have a record of what we've gone over."

He slid the file back over for Jake to return and asked him a question. "If you were a detective on that case today, what would you do?"

Jake thought about his answer before he replied, "I guess I'd want to see some surveillance footage if there was any. Check all the cameras in the vicinity to see if we find anything. Then I'd probably check his credit card purchases and get his cell records to go through his texts and calls. but other than that, I don't really know."

Spears looked satisfied with his answer but added his two cents. "On a case like this, without witnesses or a backstory to trace, cameras are about all we'd have to go off. The only other thing we often use is a victim's social media, but that can be hit or miss."

Spears got up from the table and said, "Go ahead and put the file back where you found it. Grab another one and meet me here at the table. I'm going to go up and grab another cup of coffee."

Jake couldn't help but feel a little deflated. The case had absolutely nothing they could investigate. It was an eye-opener for him. He had started the file assuming that all cold cases still had an untouched angle to work somewhere, but now he was worried it was the opposite. If this was how all the old cases were then his next few weeks were going to feel like an eternity.

Jake grabbed the file from the table and stood up. He walked back into the case room and into the fluorescent lighting that was now making a high-pitched ring. He stopped in the room and looked over the rows of cabinets.

Feeling discouraged, Jake wanted to do his best to keep an open mind. Being his first task on the new job, he felt he needed to prove he was worth the time and he wanted to start off on the right foot.

He moved over to the 1985 cabinet and opened it. Jake placed the file back where he found it and looked over the others in front of him. There were close to thirty. He understood that he had 48 other cabinets that would look similar. Jake held onto the thought that somewhere, hidden in the room, was a case waiting to be found. One that actually needed another look. As Jake stared at the files, it became apparent that in order for him to find the case he was after, he'd have to put in the time and sift through the duds.

Chapter 3

Sean was working on steadying his nerves as he watched Riverwood Police Chief, Richard Perry, field questions from the press. It was the morning after the murder of Abigail Thompson and the crime scene was beginning to circulate questions throughout Riverwood.

Sean knew he would have to speak and the idea of his name being in the papers made him more nervous than he thought it would. At the time, people got their news mainly from the local papers. Television was still a growing commodity and antennas only provided three national networks: ABC, CBS, and NBC. It wouldn't be until the late 70s that the modern T.V. dynamic would come into play.

Chief Perry looked over and gave Sean a wink. He understood that it was his turn to answer questions. The chief finished up at the podium and stepped away.

The small conference room in the new police station

was holding six reporters but to Sean, it felt more like forty. The Riverwood station had never held a press conference for a homicide before. The building had only been standing since November of 1968.

Sean got behind the podium, introduced himself and began regurgitating much of the same information Chief Perry had just laid out. The reporters looked to be growing agitated and Sean could tell they were anticipating more Q&A time. He quickly wrapped up his summary of the homicide and looked up to an eager room.

Hands shot up as he finished speaking. Sean pointed at the man sitting nearest to him. The reporter looked squirrely but had a booming voice and said, "Ed Donaldson, *Rocky Mountain News*. Do we know the business of this crime? Domestic altercations aren't usually something we see here."

Sean took no time with his answer. "We are unaware of the connection between the victim and the killer at this time but you're right, this is rare for the area."

"I haven't heard a description of the killer. Were there any witnesses?"

Sean's voice quieted. "Unfortunately, no. All we know currently is that we are dealing with a lone male assailant."

Sean looked left and pointed to the next hand. The reporter stood up to speak. "Nathan Retti, *The Denver Post*. You mentioned that Mrs. Thompson was killed by four gunshot wounds. Was your team able to retrieve a gun?"

"We did not find a gun, but we did retrieve the .45 caliber shells. The county crime lab is looking at those now and should be able to tell us exactly what type of gun was used."

Sean picked the next hand. Another reporter rose and said, "Ken Poland, with the *Riverwood Sentinel*. You mentioned that the crime happened in the garage. Was the killer also in the house?"

Sean loosened his grip on the podium and could feel his feet underneath him again. The initial shock of all the attention was wearing off, and his voice was returning. "We weren't able to determine if anything happened inside the house itself. The killer broke a pane of glass in the side door to the garage to gain access to the home. Beyond that, there isn't any conclusive evidence that tells us he moved onto another part of the house."

Ken asked a follow-up question. "Chief Perry mentioned that Mrs. Thompson appeared to be taking the trash out when the event occurred. Did it look as though the killer was there for her belongings, or her?"

"As I mentioned earlier, we were not able to determine a motive, but it did not appear that the assailant was in her garage for her car."

The reporters knew what that meant. This case was no run-of-the-mill grand theft auto gone wrong. It was intentional. The part that bothered them the most was the cold. It had gotten down to below freezing the night before. How long had this man waited in a dark garage for his victim to open the door?

Nathan Retti raised his hand again. "Has there been any peculiar behavior in the neighborhood recently?"

"Nothing out of the ordinary. Only the typical teen-age mischief. A few calls regarding minor vandalism and a couple about a peeping Tom, but nothing aggressive or overly alarming."

The reporters looked concerned. They had a murder to write about in a nice suburb outside of Denver, but they only had the basic details. All they could say for sure was that a middle-aged, divorced woman was shot in her garage by an unknown man. The rest of their story would be up to them.

The news teams began to look around the room until they realized no one else had any other questions. Sean noticed the break in the room and thanked the group for their time before stepping away from the podium. The reporters finished the last of their notes and began to file out of the room.

Sean felt as though the Q&A had gone well but he knew he would still be anxious to pick up a paper the following morning.

After the press conference, Sean walked back to his

desk and slouched into his chair. He called out across the bullpen to Carol, who was working dispatch and taking calls from the operators. "Hey Carol, have we had any more calls about the Shoshone Street murder?"

Carol's voice carried back over the bullpen from beyond the cubicles. "None that you're waiting for. Every caller has just been asking questions, no tips or witnesses yet."

Sean sighed and sunk deeper into his chair. Dave found his way over to Sean's desk and said, "You handled the press well. I think the papers know we're running the best investigation we can."

Sean didn't look up to acknowledge Dave. He was happy to be done with the press but the fact that they still didn't have a witness was eating at him and made him uncharacteristically pessimistic. Sean stared blankly at his desk and eventually replied, "I don't think I'm going to read any of them."

Dave nodded his head and tried to change the mood. "This one's a bitch. All we can do is work our way up from here and start to build the case. The body is at the coroner's and the forensics team has had time to check those shells. They'll be going through the fingerprints next and you never know, we might get lucky."

Sean still didn't feel optimistic. He knew that Dave was hoping for a fingerprint match found somewhere in the garage. One that could be linked to Abby's ex-husband. Sean, too, had been skeptical about her ex. It was common practice to examine the victim's closest relationships, but they had already spoken to the ex earlier in the morning and it was clear that he couldn't have committed the murder.

Abby's ex and the rest of the family had solid alibis. In fact, her entire background had checked out. Her coworkers were home with their families, and her friends claimed she lived a quiet life without an enemy in the world. None of it made sense to the detectives. They couldn't understand why someone wanted her dead.

Dave was still searching for the silver lining. It was usually him that Sean had to encourage along, and the reversed roles made him uneasy. He wanted to get his partner back on the horse. Dave tried his best to come up with a reasonable line of thinking to get Sean into the conversation and said, "What if he tossed the gun somewhere and we just missed it? It might be a good idea to head back over there and give it another pass through."

"We could do that. It'd be nice to have the gun, but it still wouldn't give us our guy. Even if we did find the gun, odds of it being new enough to have a serial number would have to be next to nothing."

It had only recently become federal law to print serial numbers on firearms. The *Gun Control Act* had gone into effect in October of the previous year.

Sean's pessimism was beginning to rub off on Dave

and he was growing frustrated. His enthusiasm for difficult cases had always been fragile. Fed up with Sean's attitude, Dave angrily asked, "So what do you propose? Wait until Christopher identifies the gun and then pop into a couple of gun stores with a pen and paper?"

Sean winced at the idea of shaking down gun shops. He was almost mad at Dave for suggesting it. No gun shop owner would allow himself to take on the reputation as the guy who pointed out his rougher clientele to the police. It would be business suicide. The simple fact of the matter was that even if Christopher was able to confidently tell them what type of gun killed Abigail Thompson, he still wouldn't be able to tell them what year the gun was purchased. Walking into a gun shop and asking questions would be pointless.

Sean gave Dave a disappointed look. He could tell how frustrated Dave was getting and he decided to give him some feedback before he lost Dave's interest entirely. Sean said, "If the gun angle is all we have right now then let's try to work it but let's go get Christopher's two cents first before we start scheming anything."

Dave's composure relaxed. It drove him mad when Sean kept to himself. All he needed to hear was some confirmation that they had a way forward. Once he felt they had hit a dead end, he would cave.

Sean looked back over at Dave and asked, "Christopher or the Coroner's first?"

Dave weighed the options in his head before he replied, "Coroner. Let's save the best for last. I'm not expecting anything we don't already know from the Coroner."

The body was taken to the Jefferson County Coroner's office. Its building was large and built with beige bricks that blended into the foreground of the front range around it. Like the Riverwood Police Station, it too was hidden in plain sight. It sat near a dentist's office, some small businesses and the county land grant college. The building saw plenty of action, serving as the morgue for every city west of Denver.

Not far from its steps stood another beige building where Christopher worked in the County Crime Lab. It was in these buildings, situated at the gates to the Rockies, where suburban sins were dissected and examined.

Sean and Dave made their way into the lobby of the Coroner's office. They were eager to meet with the forensic pathologist who oversaw Mrs. Thompson's autopsy. They walked past the receptionist as they had a thousand times before, flashing her their badges. Dave stated their business as they moved by.

"We're here to meet with Mark Alter."

The receptionist nodded the detectives along. They walked through two double doors and quickly found Mark. He noticed them as they came in and gestured the detectives over. Mark spoke as they came closer, "Dave, Sean, good to see you. I'll make this brief. I'm sure you guys are busy."

The detectives moved past a long row of body drawers and stopped at an open one protruding into the room. It held the body of Abigail Thompson. Mark walked around the body to a rolling table covered with papers and proceeded to hand the detectives files that he had made earlier in the morning. The file contained photographs and a write-up.

Mark was a nervous man and he tended to run through his reports in a quick ramble when he spoke to detectives. The word within local law enforcement was that he was more comfortable around cold bodies than warm ones. For that reason, he didn't keep many friends.

He waited to talk until the detectives opened the files and said, "In those files is everything we found. As you know, she was shot four times. We removed each bullet but none of them were intact. Each one had hit some sort of cartilage or bone on entry. I was able to note the cause of death as the bullet that went through her face and cut through her spinal cord. The other wounds would have made her bleed to death, but by severing the spinal cord she died rather quickly."

Sean had pulled out his notepad and was writing as Mark spoke. He tried his best to keep up as Mark continued.

"We determined her blood type to be B negative. No other blood types were found on her person or her clothes. We were also able to confirm that the victim was not sexually assaulted or involved in a struggle. Her hands and fingernails were clean, and she had no other wounds besides the gunshots."

Sean looked at his notes and realized that in his hurry his handwriting had turned into illegible scratchings and abbreviations. Dave had kept his eyes fixated on the body. He took himself out of the stare and turned to Mark to say, "Thank you, Mark. Sounds like the time of death would have been around a quarter to eight, then?"

Mark nodded. "Yeah, around then."

Sean and Dave didn't have too many questions for him. The autopsy had gone exactly as they had assumed it would. The two thanked Mark for his time and left with their files underarm.

Sean walked out of the building first and called back to Dave. "I'll let you take the notes from that guy next time. It's impossible to keep up."

"What'd you take the notes for? We didn't learn anything we didn't already know."

The two men approached the crime lab and stepped into an identical looking lobby. They both knew where Christopher's desk was and made their way up the stairs to the second floor. They had to meander around tables placed about the office space until they reached the clearing where Christopher sat.

The detectives popped down into two brown corduroy chairs in front of him. Sean started, "Is this a good time?"

Christopher looked up from some paperwork and replied, "It's always a good time. Did you already hit the morgue?"

Sean nodded and Christopher responded, "Anything I need to know?"

"No. Nothing you don't know already. There were four bullets, no sexual assault, no evidence of a struggle."

"Well, I guess that doesn't change anything for us."

Christopher leaned back in his chair and put his right arm over his head. The chair creaked loudly as he did it. "I got a little something for you guys."

Sean felt excited and leaned forward in his chair. Dave spoke up from next to Sean. "Did you match any prints?"

"No. No matches. Most of the prints were smudged."

Dave sat back in his chair, disheartened, but Sean was still holding on for the good news.

Christopher pulled out a couple of photos and pointed at them, instructing the detectives as he went along. "The pin impressions left on these shells are consistent with the markings made by a Colt M1911 .45 caliber pistol." He paused briefly and then continued.

"However, that doesn't do much for us because that happens to be the standard-issue sidearm for the entire United States Armed Forces and has been since 1911. On top of that, they were also made available to the general public back in 1950. So, there's a ton of them."

Sean rubbed his face. "So, you're saying he could be a military guy?"

"Maybe, or maybe not. Like I said, there's a lot of these."

The detectives were hoping that from talking to Christopher they could clear things up and make a plan around consolidated information but instead, it felt like they had just muddied the water.

Dave was sitting deep in his chair. After Christopher let down his fingerprint hopes and let them know that the shells wouldn't get them anywhere conclusive, he sank even lower into the corduroy. Dave asked, "So we don't have any prints and the gun used in the homicide turned out to be one of the most widely held pistols in the country?"

Christopher didn't know what else to tell them. He replied, "I'm sorry, guys. Bad hand."

Sean and Dave were both disappointed. Since they had started on the case the night before, they only seemed to be finding dead ends. With the way the homicide was going they were worried they'd have to rely on witnesses and called-in tips, both of which had been scarce thus far. But they expected the next morning's newspapers would churn up a buzz around the homicide and give the case more attention.

The detectives thanked Christopher for his time. Their day wasn't working out as they had hoped but they couldn't give up yet.

Dave had become cynical about Christopher's update on the prints during the drive back. His attitude was stressing Sean out, he needed to hear some good news if they had any. Stepping back into the Riverwood Station, Sean walked over to Carol, who was still behind the front desk.

"Hey Carol, got any calls for us about Shoshone?" asked Sean in a monotone voice.

"The *Rocky Mountain News* called to—"

Sean cut her off abruptly by putting a hand in the air and said, "Any *witness* calls?"

Carol looked startled by the interruption. "No, sorry Sean."

Sean brought his hand down on her desk and knocked it lightly. He slowly moved past her back towards his desk. His monotone voice remained. "Thanks, Carol."

The detectives strolled into the bullpen and dropped their briefcases. Sean crashed into his well-worn office chair. Dave took a seat in his and rubbed his forehead.

It was nearing the end of the day and he didn't have it in him to continue thinking about the case. He looked over at Sean and said, "It's been a rough one."

Sean sighed, "Yes, it has."

Dave looked down at his briefcase with a feeling of disgust. "God damn, I'm beat."

Sean didn't respond.

Dave could see the stress and exhaustion in his partner's posture. The day hadn't gone as planned and they had both taken turns feeling sorry for themselves. Their emotions seemed to be leading them in circles and Dave was suddenly guilty about letting his feelings get the best of him in the car. With the weight they were under, he again worried about Sean losing hope in the case. Dave took a break from his attitude and attempted to lighten the mood. He asked, "Have you had anything to eat today?"

"No, I don't think I have."

Dave smiled back at Sean. "I don't think I have, either. You want to slip over next door and grab some pancakes?"

Dave was closely watching Sean's face to see if the idea of food would cheer him up. Not getting the response he wanted, he kept at it. "I get it if you have dinner plans with your lady tonight but if you don't, pancakes and eggs fix everything."

Both their wives knew that they couldn't expect their

husbands home at a reasonable hour a day after a murder. The detectives always became too involved in the cases and usually had to stay late.

Sean looked up at Dave through narrow eyes. Food did sound good, but he knew the real reason Dave loved the Ralston Cafe. Sean said, "You're just trying to hit on that waitress again."

Dave gave Sean his best confused look. "Who? The owner's daughter? I mean, she's cute but come on, pancakes sound good."

Sean laughed. Dave was happily married with kids but for some reason, he got a kick out of trying to flirt with the waitress. For Sean, it was harmless entertainment. Dave's jokes never landed, and the waitress always seemed to be in a bad mood. There were times when it was more satisfying watching Dave's jokes crash than actually eating the food.

Sean straightened up in his chair and looked back at Dave. He replied, "Alright. I could do some pancakes."

Dave was glad to see Sean's attitude improve. He couldn't stand the idea of looking over the evidence again and he was always content to switch his mind over from work to pancakes.

The detectives stepped out of the station and into a cold February night. The smell of moisture occupied the usually dry air. It was the warning of an incoming snowstorm. Hurrying over to the Ralston Cafe, the smell of moisture was overpowered by the smells of maple syrup and bacon.

After they took two steps through the door a waitress started clearing off their usual table. Sean's attitude immediately began to improve, and he let himself relax. Allowing himself a break from the stress in the heat of the chaos always helped keep his head on his shoulders.

Dave took the conversation back over to the waitress once they took their seats. "Think she's working tonight?"

Sean gave him the grin he wanted and replied, "Josephine works the weekdays, so I'd assume so."

"She goes by Josie, man. No one calls her Josephine."

Sean was already amused by Dave. He could tell that the new environment was having an impact on his partner as well. Sean decided to play along with him and said, "Well the only thing she'll be getting from you is your order."

Dave laughed off Sean's joke with a "screw off," and they both waited for Josie.

She walked through the kitchen door with two coffees and set them on their table. Josie barely acknowledged them as she said, "Two decaf coffees because it's after six."

Dave had a smile on his face and Sean could tell that he was trying to think of something clever to reply with. He eventually muttered, "Thanks for looking out for us,

Josie, somebody has to. If my kids found out I was allowed caffeine after twelve, there'd be a riot."

Josie halfheartedly smiled, clearly trying to avoid further conversation, and moved on to their orders. She asked, "You both having the same thing again?"

Sean replied, "Yeah, I am. Two eggs over easy, pancakes, bacon and a water, too." Dave nodded in agreement and Josie walked back to the kitchen.

Once she was out of earshot, Sean ripped into Dave. "Wow, was that a caffeine joke?"

Dave brushed him off and lit a cigarette. He sat back as he said, "It's late for her. She's been here all day and she's tired. No one likes to small talk when they're tired."

Dave took a couple of drags from his cigarette and got to his coffee. Sean played with the creamer as his mind drifted back to the case. He couldn't let the break last long. "No prints, no witnesses, no nothing. We might have pulled a dud."

Dave shook his head and focused on his cigarette as he replied, "Let's just let it sit for a little, alright? I need a break."

Sean settled back into his seat and sighed. "What I can't wrap my head around is *why*. Where's the motive?"

Dave knew there was no way out of the conversation. Once Sean got going, he was hard to stop. Dave ashed the butt of his cigarette and looked over at his partner. "I don't know, maybe she owed money to someone. After all, she was a single woman with bills to pay. Life ain't cheap, and It's hard on one income."

"You think she was messing with loan sharks?"

"Always a possibility."

Sean nodded. "I agree. It's possible, but if it was a back-pay issue, I think they would have dealt with it the way most of them do. We would have found her in a field, not her garage."

The smell of butter and bacon stole their attention. Josie came back through the kitchen door and placed two plates on the table. "Alright guys, here it is. Enjoy."

Sean grabbed the syrup and poured it on his pancakes. As he looked over his food his mind wandered back to the press conference. He asked, "What do you think they're going to say about us in the paper? That Ed always has a way with words."

Dave was already working on his pancakes. Between bites, he got out a muffled, "Just eat your damn food."

It was pitch black out by the time the detectives finished eating. The smell of moisture lingered in the air outside, but it was now accompanied by a light snowfall that dusted the parking lot and stuck to windshields.

Dave called out to Sean as they went their separate ways. "I'll catch you in the morning." Sean waved back and hustled over to his car parked in front of the station. He was looking forward to getting to sleep. He'd barely slept the night before. Once he was turned on to a new case, it was hard for him to turn off his internal chatter. He'd wake himself up every hour worried about what he hadn't thought of, but it never did him any good. Sean prayed they wouldn't get another homicide stacked up on them. They were still on call for the rest of the week and having to think about two murders would be overwhelming.

He got to his 1968 Plymouth Belvedere, wiped the snow off his windows, climbed inside and started the engine. As the car warmed up, he lit a cigarette. He liked to smoke after he ate. It usually leveled him out and got his mind working. Tonight, he needed the buzz to overcome his exhaustion and help get him home.

Sean rolled the car out of the parking lot and started down the street. Traffic was light for the night, but he kept hitting red lights. He pulled in front of a red at his fourth traffic stop and realized he was at the intersection that turned into Abigail Thompson's neighborhood. Sean let the light go green while he sat at the intersection. The rush from his cigarette was fighting the fog of his fatigue but his curiosity came through. Dave and Sean hadn't returned to the crime scene that day and for some reason, he wanted another look at the house. He turned right and headed down the street.

He drove until he got to the intersection with Shoshone and took a left. He slowed the car down and pulled it over to the curb on the opposite side of the street. Sean killed the engine and turned off the lights. He sat in his car and stared at the house.

The neighborhood looked peaceful in the falling snow. Snowflakes stuck to the lights, making the dark street a shade deeper. The streetlights on the block had caused Sean a lot of headache. He blamed them for the lack of even a basic description of the man he was after.

He looked harder across the street at the dark house, closed his eyes and mentally walked through the crime scene again. He opened them and looked back at the house through the snow. Nothing was coming to mind.

The quiet setting of the snow falling on his car was putting him to sleep. His weariness clouded his memory and he knew it'd be better to revisit the case in the morning. He turned the key over in the ignition and flipped his car lights back on. The street illuminated in front of him and his eye caught a silhouette he hadn't noticed before. It was standing just beyond the range of the streetlight at the next intersection. The figure didn't seem to be moving. Sean waited for the man to do something for the scene to look normal, but the moment passed.

His gaze was transfixed.

The silhouette remained and appeared to be watching him. The hairs on the back of Sean's neck slowly began to stand. He put the car in drive, never breaking his stare. As his foot touched the accelerator the man turned and ran down the adjacent street.

Startled, Sean let his foot off the accelerator and thought to himself, *What the hell was that?* His heart kicked into a beat, and his eyes searched the snow-covered street corner.

He looked over to his glove compartment and grabbed his model 28 pistol. He quickly checked if it was loaded and put his eyes back on the corner.

The figure was gone.

He rolled his window down, put the pistol on his lap and hit the gas. Sean turned the corner where he saw the man disappear. His headlights lit up a deserted street. He yelled to himself, "Shit!" He slowed the car to a roll and crept down the street. His mind scrambled for answers as he talked to himself, "Did I really just see that?"

He drove up to the next intersection and stopped the car. He couldn't see anything but empty streets from the intersection. He looked over at the snow-covered sidewalk and looked for tracks.

He couldn't see any.

Sean put the car in reverse and turned on his side-light. He faced the light out towards the sidewalk and backed up the car. He went slowly until his eyes caught the man's footprints. He stopped the car and adjusted the sidelight to see where the tracks had gone. It lit up one of the many entrances to the ditch trail that wound through the neighborhood.

Sean didn't know what to do. He sat in his car staring down the dark path hoping his eyes would adjust to the night. His car's side light barely penetrated the trail. Sean stared at the park entrance for a few seconds until he snapped out of it and put the car back in drive. He drove up to the intersection and turned down the next street driving parallel to the ditch trail. He got to another intersection and turned back towards the trail hoping to cut the man off.

He pulled the car to a stop in front of the trail and put his sidelight down it. He looked around the sidewalk and saw the man's footprints already underneath his car, he was too late. The man had already crossed here. Sean put the car back into drive and turned onto Shoshone, driving parallel to the ditch trail again. He drove until the street came unexpectedly to a cul-de-sac. He looked around for another entrance to the ditch trail but couldn't find one. He yelled to himself again, "Son of a bitch."

Now feeling paranoid, his eyes scanned the snow-covered street. Whomever he was following had gotten away in the ditch trail. He pulled the car around the cul-de-sac and started back towards Abigail Thompson's house. He drove slowly while his mind continued to race for an explanation of what had just occurred. Yet, regardless of the scenarios he played in his head, he couldn't rationalize the situation. He tried to tell himself he could have been following anyone, but he didn't believe it. He was doing everything he could to avoid the creeping feeling that the man he had just seen, was the same one he was after.

Chapter 4
2018

It was 6:00 a.m. on a Friday when Chief Kelly walked through the front doors of the police station. He was headed straight to the breakroom to get his morning cup of coffee when he stopped, confused to see his new detective already at his desk. Surprised, he asked, "What are you doing here so early? Aren't you still going through cold cases with Spears?"

It was the end of Jake's second week and Kelly wasn't expecting to see him in before seven. By the second week of cold cases, most detectives lose interest and start begging to be turned out to the field. Kelly figured Jake was in early to get him alone and plead his case. The chief cut Jake off before he could respond, "If you're here to say you want to start working in the field with Julie, I understand but I'm leaving it up to Captain Spears."

Jake returned a questioning look. Kelly could tell that

he had misread the situation and asked, "You're not here to ask to be turned out to the field?"

Jake shook his head.

Now the chief was more confused. If Jake was here to work on cold cases, then he was the first new detective Kelly had seen who was this eager to jump into old paperwork. He knew something had to be up. The young detective looked alert and excited.

Jake asked him, "How much do you keep up to date with the news?"

Kelly didn't know what that meant. He didn't pay much attention to television and he had stopped watching the news ever since the last presidential election. He replied, "Not a lot. I don't care too much about politics. The kids keep me on Netflix. What's up?"

Jake's eyes widened. He struggled with how to break the news. Kelly asked him again, "Well, what happened?"

Jake proudly replied, "They caught the Golden State Killer in California."

After he said it, Jake was expecting to see a reaction from Kelly, but the chief clearly didn't know the weight of the situation. Kelly responded, "Who the hell is the Golden State Killer?"

Jake had assumed everyone knew who the maniac was at this point. The news was breaking all over the country. Jake explained, "He was a serial killer and rapist who had over fifty unsolved cases going back to the seventies. The case was cold until last week when they arrested the guy. I saw an article about it last night and it's all over T.V. today."

"Oh. Good for them. How'd they do it, updates with the DNA evidence?"

Jake nodded.

Kelly's expression hadn't changed. It seemed as though he had heard the story a thousand times. He turned and started back for the break room, saying out loud, "That CODIS is something else. It always makes me smile when they catch one."

"That's the crazy part. They didn't catch him with CODIS."

Kelly stopped and turned back around. "How'd they do it, then?"

"The internet. They used a free ancestry website to link the DNA they had from their crime scenes to a relative of the guy."

Kelly's jaw dropped.

Jake smiled, "Yeah, I know. It's crazy."

The chief said it back to Jake to make sure he heard it right. "They tracked down their guy from one of his relatives on the internet?"

Jake nodded and Kelly shook his head in disbelief. He asked, "Is that legal? That's insane."

"I had the same reaction."

"Shit, that could be a game-changer." The chief

continued shaking his head and turned back for the breakroom.

Once Kelly had walked away, Jake went back to impatiently waiting at his desk for Spears to get in. *The Sacramento Bee* article he had read the night before was all he could think about. The story read like fiction, but it only covered the general aspects of the case and Jake needed to know more. From what he had picked up, it all centered around a free website called GEDmatch but what he wanted to know was how they used it. If it was something that could be easily done, then what was stopping him from doing the same thing with one of Riverwood's cases?

Jake figured Spears or Julie would be coming in early, too. He couldn't have been the only one that saw the news. He looked around the dead station and decided his time would be better spent rereading the article. He took out his phone and pulled up *The Sacramento Bee*.

The story detailed how a county investigative team had exhausted all their efforts in identifying the Golden State Killer, but through one last-ditch effort pulled off a miracle. They created a profile on the website GEDmatch and uploaded their killer's DNA. GEDmatch functions as a popular genealogists' tool built to connect families and identify unknown relatives. Luckily for the investigators, the Golden State Killer had a distant relative who had created an account. Recognizing that the cousin shared paternal DNA with the Golden State Killer, the investigative team had a genetic genealogist work through the cousin's paternal family tree in an attempt to identify a common male ancestor between the cousin and the Golden State Killer.

Once the genealogist had settled on multiple potential ancestors, they then had to work down the family trees branching from those ancestors to produce a suspect field. This created a large list of living and deceased suspects who had access to the Golden State Killer's areas of operation during his active time. It was only after a long process of elimination that the investigative team was finally able to identify their man by collecting a swab of his DNA off his car door.

Jake finished the article and put his phone away. Even after reading the story again, he still couldn't believe it himself. As the morning slowly crept along, more people began to trickle into the station. Jake couldn't resist wanting to gossip. He got up to get a cup of coffee and fill the others in on the news.

The story spread quickly around the Riverwood station. Jake spent most of his early morning talking to everyone in earshot about the case. For the last two weeks, he had been going over cold cases with Spears, but they only seemed to be reviewing duds. Not one case had given him much inspiration, but this news story had stolen his attention. Jake understood that this California cold case was the start of something big. It was as though the investigative team had made their man's name appear out of thin air. DNA evidence had taken on a new definition, essentially overnight. It now had the ability to turn any unknown offender into a known suspect. Practically every officer in the station agreed with Chief Kelly, this was a game-changer. It marked the largest advancement in police forensics since DNA first broke the scene in the U.S. back in 1988 with the Southside Strangler case in Virginia.

CODIS was an incredible tool but it only allowed law enforcement to look within a certain pool of individuals. With GEDmatch, investigators had the whole sea. The website was still growing but if it could reach only a few million uploads then genealogists would have the ability to identify practically anyone in the United States.

Jake wondered how many cases had passed through CODIS without a hit. Cases where investigators were so painfully close to solving them but still came up empty-handed. Now, with GEDmatch, those cases had a second chance.

Jake was back at his desk, searching for more articles on his phone when he heard Spears's voice over the bullpen. He made his way over to the captain's office and let himself inside. Spears was still dropping his bags when

Jake walked in. The captain looked up and acknowledged him. "I thought you'd be here early."

"You saw the article too?"

Spears widened his eyes and nodded. Jake rushed over and took a seat in front of his desk. The young detective blurted out, "Can you believe this shit? I can't take my eyes off the news."

"I still don't know if I *do* believe it. It doesn't seem real, but it makes sense."

Jake was happy that Spears was up to speed. He had waited all morning to talk to him about the story and to hear what he thought it meant for their cold cases. "This changes everything," he said. "I mean, should we go through our old unidentified rape kits to see if we can get some new results?"

Spears rubbed his head. He had assumed Jake would ask these questions after he saw the story. He thought about the question and then replied, "We could. But remember, it has to be both a sexual assault and a murder if the case is older than twenty years."

Jake had forgotten about the statute of limitations. He countered back to Spears. "What about just murder cases then? Older cases that, before, would have been overlooked. Cases that we could now give another shot."

The captain could see the passion in Jake's eyes. What his young detective was proposing was an ambitious amount of work, but he agreed with him, it was an exciting possibility. Just the idea of it gave him goose-bumps. Spears leveled with Jake and said, "Well first off, if we did pull a legitimate DNA profile out of an older case, we'd still run it through CODIS. Secondly, looking for DNA in older murder cases won't be easy and there's no sure way that we will find a legitimate deposit. Our biggest issue would be proving that the DNA we'd find actually belonged to the murderer."

Jake understood what the captain was saying. They would somehow have to make sure there was a chance the cases they were reviewing had some of the offender's DNA in the remaining evidence. Proving that the DNA they would ultimately find actually belonged to the killer would be another hurdle, but Jake felt inspired. He was done picking cases at random. He now wanted to start from the beginning, pull the files all the way back from 1969 and give every single one a fresh look until he found the case he was after. A case he could test for DNA and throw into CODIS and eventually GEDmatch.

The young detective mulled over the captain's reality check before replying, "Say we do end up finding a case that we want to put into GEDmatch. Would that even be a possibility for us?"

"We have some great criminologists at the county lab. If it can be done, I have no doubts that they could figure it out."

Jake leaned forward in his chair. "I think we should

try. What else are we looking at these old cases for anyway than to give them another chance?"

Jake's determination was convincing, and Spears didn't necessarily hate the idea. He was just as excited about the news as Jake was. The captain thought to himself that if the DA wanted this young detective to go over cold cases before his field experience, then he'd make sure Jake got a good education. He was willing to give the new method a shot. The young man would gain invaluable experience, and in the process, they would get the chance to make a difference in a case that had been long forgotten.

Spears looked back over at Jake and said, "Ok. I agree. Let's see what we can do but like I said, this isn't going to be easy."

Chapter 5
1969

Kathrine Sandoval was home alone. She had just finished dinner with her husband, John, before he left
for night school, something he had been doing weekly
since the beginning of the year. As usual, she had settled
into the couch for NBC's *Rowan & Martin's Laugh-In*, her
favorite comedy show, which she watched every Monday
night. She had a show for every night of the week, but
Mondays were her favorite. The comedic relief helped
her cope with the loneliness that crept up on her when
her husband was away. Comedy had always been how she
dealt with things. Whether it was a bad day at work or
just a day gone wrong, she knew that somehow there was
probably a joke about it.

Like most people, Kathy had routines. She lived a
daily schedule, but she made sure that no matter how the
day panned out she'd stick to her two unbreakable habits:
what she ate for lunch and how she spent her weeknights.

Always a tuna sandwich and always NBC by eight. The only pause she allowed herself once she sat down in front of the T.V. was to curb her craving for smoking cigarettes. Kathy had been a smoker since she was fifteen and during commercial breaks, she would try to sneak out to the garage for a cigarette. She and John had started smoking in the garage ever since his brother had a baby. The family came over more often and they didn't want their nephew breathing bad air.

The commercials came right on cue. Kathy got up, grabbed her pack of cigarettes off the kitchen counter and headed for the garage. She needed to burn one down before the show came back. Hurriedly, she stepped in front of the door and reached for the handle but stopped. She'd forgotten her pack of lights in the kitchen drawer. She walked back to the kitchen to fetch the matches and made sure to turn the volume up on the T.V. so she could hear it from in the garage. If she heard the show starting back up, she would put out her cigarette and run to the couch. It was a fun game she played with herself to see if she could time it right. With the matches in hand, she hustled back to the garage door and pushed it open.

Stepping into the garage, the door closed behind her. Kathy reached out for the light switch as she had a hundred times before. Her hand instinctively found it and flipped the switch. It echoed in the empty garage. The sound lingered but the light didn't respond. Calmly, she tried it again. Once more she had the same result. This wasn't her first time working around the inconvenience of a burnt-out bulb. She could get by with the matches. She fumbled with her pack of smokes, trying to find the open end, and pulled out a cigarette. She snapped off a match from the bundle and put the cigarette to her mouth.

Holding the matchbox in one hand and the match in the other, Kathy struck the match off the pack. She pulled the lit match in front of her face. Her eyes were immediately drawn to its intense light. As quickly as the match had lit, it sputtered out. She'd have to try another.

She was worried that she was taking too long. She could still hear the television roaring through her garage door, but two commercials had just finished. Kathy knew she only had a couple of minutes before the show was back on. She dropped the burnt match and pulled out one more. This time she was a little quicker. She struck the match and brought it swiftly to her cigarette. She took deep drags and focused on the burning cherry it produced. She watched it glow coal red until she was satisfied. Kathy pulled the cigarette away from her face and blew out the smoke.

A calm came over her, she knew she'd make it back in time for the show.

Kathy looked towards the match as she shook it out and her hair raised. The match went out leaving her in the dark, but the pair of men's shoes that she saw were only visible for a brief second.

She looked towards them in the blacked-out garage unable to see anything besides her burning cigarette. What on earth were those shoes doing there?

She took another drag and the cherry bloomed, illuminating her face. The T.V. was still screaming from the other side of the door. Kathy smoked and stood in silence, wondering what her husband's shoes were doing in the garage. He only had one pair like the ones she had seen, and he was wearing them.

She pulled out another match from the box and struck it. It kicked off the smell of sulfur as it breathed to life. She held it out towards the shoes near the back of the garage and her stomach dropped.

The shoes led to a flickering silhouette standing in them. The man in the corner was silent, holding a knife and staring with a grim expression. His eyes were transfixed on her. Kathy could only stare back. The match burned closer to its stem until it went out.

~ ~ ~

It had been a long nine weeks since the murder of Abigail Thompson. Sean never knew what to make of his night outside of her house after the murder. The more he tried to remember what happened, the more the memory seemed to blend into a bad dream. It didn't feel real. He never told Dave about it. He had no idea where to begin if he did. Just the thought of trying to explain chasing a shadowed figure through the snowy streets of Riverwood seemed ridiculous. Sean knew if he even attempted, he'd never hear the end of it. No one would believe him anyway, so he figured he was better off keeping it to himself.

The case had gone cold soon after. In the time since, Sean had lost all hope in waiting for a break in the case. He had moved on and written it off as a loss weeks ago. Dave hadn't even hung on that long. Just a week after the murder he was already putting his mind on other things.

The city had quickly forgotten the murder, too. People downplayed Abby's story as a strange irregularity and rumors circled about her private life. Everyone in town had their own explanations for the homicide. The only remembrance left behind from the shooting was the for-sale sign in front of Abby's house. Once that was gone, the memory would be buried with her body and left to her family.

Sean and Dave got back to business as usual. They'd been assigned another homicide a few weeks earlier. One that had a clear-cut motive and led them into familiar territory. The story of Abigail Thompson was on its way to being forgotten.

So, when the detectives got a call about another murder in a residential garage on a week when they weren't on call, they had mixed feelings about it. But they both agreed that they at least owed it a look.

The detectives stepped onto the fresh crime scene at 4545 Routt Way at 10:38 p.m. They had been called in by their lieutenant to work with fellow detectives Bobby Hull and Steve Vincinni.

Sean and Dave made their way up to the door of the house and walked inside. There they found Vincinni sitting on the living room couch. He got up to greet them. "Sorry you guys had to come out, but we all agreed you had to look at this. It appears to be an exact copy of what you had back in February."

Vincinni walked them through the house and over to the open door that led to the garage. Christopher was standing on the other side, his flashlight pointed at what the detectives assumed was a body. They could see wiped up blood all over the floor. Christopher looked up to Sean and Dave. "Sorry you guys had to come out here tonight," he said, "but this is a déjà vu."

Dave stepped into the garage and looked down at the body. The poor woman had been stabbed repeatedly. The garage smelled of cigarettes, but the air had a metallic taste from the blood that covered everything.

Christopher stepped back to allow the detectives into the garage. He briefed them as they gathered in over the body. "Our victim is twenty-nine-year-old Kathrine Sandoval. As you can see, she suffered multiple stab wounds." Christopher led his flashlight from the body to the side door of the garage. "Just like Shoshone, the attacker broke in through the side door leading into the garage and once again, we don't have an overhead light."

Sean pulled out his notebook and looked around the garage. He had a bad feeling growing in his stomach. They had inferred that Abigail Thompson's killer planned the murder, but seeing the same methods applied to another victim made him worry they were onto something bigger. They downplayed the missing light from Shoshone as happenstance. It never made the paper and was something that only the killer would have known about. Now it appeared that it was part of the plan. From two seconds in the garage, Sean and Dave understood why their lieutenant called them out. The murder they were looking at could have only been committed by the same lunatic.

Sean asked the room, "When did this happen?"

"Sometime between seven-thirty and nine-thirty. Her husband claimed to have found her when he got back from night school," answered Vincinni.

"Is he still here?"

"He's in the backyard with Lieutenant Harrison."

Christopher pointed his flashlight back at the body and said, "Nothing was taken from the house, her husband had the car and her clothes weren't removed. It's the exact same scenario as the Shoshone murder but with one major difference, the murder weapon."

Sean didn't want to look at the body for too long. It was disfigured and riddled with stab wounds. Christopher bent down near the body and lifted one of her hands.

"You can tell just by looking at her that this didn't go easy. She's got skin and blood under her fingernails. She didn't go without a fight."

Vincinni looked over to the broken door and asked, "Did you get any prints off of the door?"

Christopher responded, "We're going to try. We didn't get anywhere with them at the Shoshone house but hopefully, we can get one that matches what we pulled there back in February." Christopher paused, remembering something else. He pointed back toward the broken door. "There are footprints on the outside of that door. The ground's finally soft enough."

Dave perked up from behind Sean and asked, "Are they pretty distinct?"

"A couple are. You can go look at them. There's more than one, so they're not too reliable but we are going to take note of them."

Sean turned his mind back to the murder weapon. "So, he used a knife this time and avoided the noise from a gun. On our last garage murder, we didn't have any solid witnesses. Have you guys canvassed the neighborhood?"

Detective Hull shook his head. "We haven't hit any doors yet. Hopefully, we get something. With the way she looks, this couldn't have been quiet."

Sean thought there could be a chance that Hull was right, but he wasn't going to count on it. He would be happy to let Vincinni and Hull take on the neighborhood for statements, but he knew that Dave and he would be knocking on doors too. He wasn't looking forward to it. Dave asked another question. "What about the husband? He didn't see anything?"

"Let's go talk to him," replied Vincinni.

As the detectives made their way to the backyard, Vincinni tapped Sean on the shoulder. "This guy is all torn up about this as you'd expect, so we didn't have much luck with him earlier. Maybe the lieutenant leveled him out, but he was in a lot of shock."

The group stepped out into the back yard. Lieutenant Harrison was sitting at a picnic table next to a man with sullen eyes. The lieutenant nodded at the detectives. "Gentleman, this is Pat Sandoval. He owns the house."

Pat didn't look up at the detectives he kept his eyes on the picnic table. Sean walked over and took a seat on the other side of the table and said, "Mr. Sandoval, I'm sorry for your loss."

Sean waited for the man to acknowledge him. When he didn't, Sean continued. "It's imperative that you tell us everything you know. Everything that happened before you left for school and when you got back."

Pat's eyes still didn't leave the table. He couldn't look at Sean. Just when Sean was about to ask him again, he started to speak. "We had dinner and I left at seven-thirty."

Sean waited for him to explain more. He tried to encourage Pat to keep talking. "That's good Mr. Sandoval. What was your wife doing when you left?"

"Watching T.V. She would always put something on when I leave."

"Do you have class every night?"

The man nodded.

Sean thought of another question. "What would your wife have been doing in the garage?"

Pat folded his arms. He still didn't break his stare on the table. "Smoking. We smoke in the garage, so the house doesn't smell. She likes to do it during commercial breaks."

Sean looked over at Dave. Just like Shoshone, this murder seemed so coincidental. Abigail Thompson had been taking out the trash and now Kathrine Sandoval had just gone out for a smoke. Sean looked back at Pat. "Mr. Sandoval, When you found your wife did you see anyone else around the house? Maybe someone on the street when you were driving home?"

Pat shook his head.

Sean didn't know what else to ask. He knew it would be hard to get something useful. He thought of the last question that came to mind. "Did anyone ever make a threat on your life? Has anybody been harassing you or your wife?"

Again, Pat shook his head.

Out of questions, Sean got up from the table. Lieutenant Harrison told Pat to wait and got up to talk to the detectives in private. They walked back into the house. Harrison started talking as soon as they were inside. "We have every available patrol car out right now looking for a lone, young, male. That's all we had as a description from Shoshone. If the guy didn't change clothes, then he would be covered in blood, but I doubt he's that stupid. We need you guys to get some statements from the neighbors. We can't put too much faith in the patrols with such a vague description."

Sean and Dave looked over at Vincinni and Hull. If they split up the houses, they could get through the neighborhood faster. Dave replied to Harrison, "Did you ask him if he or his wife knew Abigail Thompson?"

"I did, and he didn't. He said he read about her in the paper, but they didn't know her."

They were all on the same page. If something could connect these two women together then that would be their starting point. The detectives left Harrison to return to Pat Sandoval and stepped outside of the house. The coroner's truck was loading up the body and taking it away. Dave looked over at Vincinni and Hull. "We'll go right if you go left. I say we hit up to two houses away and then cross the street. After that, we can try the houses behind them."

Vincinni nodded, and he and Hull went on their way.

Dave looked over to Sean and said, "Well, here we go again."

Sean crashed into his desk chair anticipating a long day. Their morning press conference hadn't gone well. Not knowing the answers to most of the questions directed at him made him uneasy. Sean could see that the reporters were picking up on his nervous demeanor. The press conference didn't seem as innocent as the one they held back in February. Even after all the reassurances they gave, the worried looks didn't change.

Sean wondered how hard the press would run with the story. He felt guilty that they didn't have the outcome they wanted, and he was concerned that the police were going to take the blame. A story like this was something a reporter could turn into a frenzy.

The night before hadn't gone well either. Just as Sean suspected, they didn't find a witness. Instead, they wasted an hour knocking on doors and scaring neighbors. Just like the case of Abigail Thompson, Kathrine Sandoval's friends and family were stunned and appalled. No immediate people of interest surfaced, and they were faced with another long shot.

Sean and Dave were exhausted. The late-night had bled into an early morning and the day didn't seem like it was going to slow down. Dave settled into his desk near Sean. He could see that Sean had a troubled mind and spoke to him out of sympathy. "Like always you handled that as best as you could. Don't beat yourself up about it."

Sean gave Dave a thankful nod and went back into his thoughts. Dave could tell that it wasn't just the press conference that Sean was struggling over. He wanted to know what it was. Dave asked, "What's up?"

"How long do you think he was in that garage?"

"I don't know."

"It was below freezing on the night Abigail Thompson died, and Kathrine Sandoval was having a smoke break. Both women didn't plan on being in the garage long and yet it seems as if the killer knew that." Sean shook his head. "I don't believe for a second that he spent all day in Abigail Thompson's garage back in February. I think he knew when both women were going to be there."

Dave didn't know how to reply. He thought about what Sean was saying before he responded, "So, you're thinking the killer knew both Abigail and Kathrine even though they didn't know each other?"

"He had to have. How else could he have known their schedules? How else could he have timed the murders right?"

It made sense to Dave, but it didn't add up. He responded, "If he knew them then why didn't he go in the house? If they both knew who he was they would have let him in, right?"

It was a good point and it made Sean unsure of his reasoning. He shook his head, "I don't know. I'm hoping time will tell."

"Hopefully so. We've let the county guys have enough time this morning, don't you think? Maybe Christopher or Mark have something for us."

Sean got up from his desk. "Let's head over there. I don't feel like waiting around here for the phones to start ringing."

The detectives went to the crime lab first. They walked up to Christopher's desk, but he wasn't there. They decided to wait him out and took a seat. After a few minutes, he came into view summiting the stairs. He waved at the detectives and made it over to his desk. As he sat down Christopher said, "You guys don't like phone calls?"

Sean shook his head. "It's better getting out of the station and you're easier to understand in person."

Christopher smiled and got right to the point. "Good news or bad news?"

Dave butted in. "Bad news."

Christopher began, "We didn't get a match with any of the prints we pulled between the Thompson house or the Sandoval house."

Dave asked, "What else?"

"The shoe sizes we got from the footprints outside

were a men's size ten, nine and seven — or a woman's eight-and-a-half. Did anyone ever find any abandoned bloodied clothing?"

Sean shook his head and Dave asked another question. "What about the knife? We had a military gun for Abigail. Is there such a thing as a military knife?"

"There is a standard-issue military knife. It's called a Ka-Bar. I haven't talked to Mark yet so I don't know the dimensions of the knife that was used but you guys can ask. A Ka-Bar is seven inches long, an eighth of an inch thick and an inch wide with a fixed blade. It has a twenty-degree angle on the tip as well. You guys haven't seen Mark yet, right?"

Dave wrote the dimensions down and responded, "We'll ask. Anything else?"

"No. That's it."

Dave closed his notebook and the detectives got up. Sean said to Christopher as they walked away, "We'll keep you in the loop."

Sean and Dave stepped inside the coroner's office next. They made their way to the autopsy rooms and passed through a pair of double doors leading to where Mark was working. He noticed them enter and gestured them over as he walked over to a body drawer and opened it up. Sean and Dave made it over and were once again looking at the body of Kathrine Sandoval.

Dave pulled out his notepad and without any other introduction, Mark began. "We confirmed that she wasn't sexually assaulted. She was stabbed nineteen times and the fatal blow appears to be the gash on her jugular. She bled out. The cuts are deep. These were all very forceful. You can see bruising around most of them." Mark was pointing at the body as he went along. "I noted the time of death around 8 p.m. and we confirmed her blood type to be A positive. We did a couple of tests, but we only recovered A positive blood."

Dave was struggling to keep up on his notepad. Sean got a kick out of watching him frantically write. Dave stopped Mark, hoping to get more time to catch up. He continued writing as he asked, "How big was this knife? What are the dimensions?"

"We measured the knife to be around eight inches long, an inch and a half wide and roughly an eighth of an inch in thickness. The blade had a straight edge that tapered to the tip. Which happens to be the common dimensions of your everyday chef's knife or household kitchen knife. Just like the one you probably got at home."

The detectives felt indifferent about the dimensions. The knife didn't rule out if their suspect was a military man or not. Their evidence was still too vague to put together an accurate profile of who their killer could be.

Mark looked back over his notes to see if he had

anything else for the detectives. He handed them copies of his report and said, "That's all I have for you guys today."

The detectives grabbed the files and put them under their arms. Their visits to Mark and Christopher hadn't given them the peace of mind they had hoped for. They thanked Mark for his time and went back on their way.

A full day passed. The detectives were now on day two after the murder of Kathrine Sandoval.

Back in his desk chair at the Riverwood station, Sean rubbed the bridge of his nose, hoping it would relieve the pain from the headache he had. The stress of the story coming out in the papers was getting to him and on top of that, he hadn't slept the night before. Every time he was about to fall asleep, he'd see the memory of the shadowed man standing in the snow outside of Abigail Thompson's house. He couldn't shake the idea that the killer would return to Kathrine Sandoval's and he had gotten out of bed twice to drive his car down to 4545 Routt way. Both times he killed the engine and watched the neighborhood with his pistol on his lap until the radio lulled him to sleep. He never saw anything, but he now hated the song "Yellow Submarine" by the Beatles.

It was still stuck in his head as Carol walked past on her way to the break room and saw him rubbing his nose. "You're in early. Have you read the paper yet?"

Sean gave her a friendly smile but shook his head. Carol kept talking as she walked into the break room. "It was pretty dramatic. You'll have to read it."

The comment made Sean nervous. He called back to Carol, "Which paper?"

"The *Rocky Mountain News*."

Sean didn't want to get ahead of himself, but he already felt mad. He knew Ed Donaldson of the *Rocky Mountain News* always put an artistic touch on his stories. What small interest Sean had in reading the paper boiled away. He was too tired and had too much angst as it was. If Ed's story really was dramatic, then he knew they were going to have a busy switchboard. He and the other detectives would have to sift through phone call after phone call, listening to stories and concerns. Sean tried to calm himself down and prepare for the day.

The morning went by quickly and much of the day was beginning to turn into a blur. Sean's fears over the *Rocky Mountain News* Article had come to fruition. He and the other detectives had been taking calls all day. They'd fielded a few phone calls after the murder of Abigail Thompson, but now after Kathrine Sandoval, they were getting swamped. Ed's article terrified most of the city and most likely gave the killer the recognition he was after.

Close to lunchtime, Dave had had enough. He got up and started to walk away. Sean yelled after him,

"Where are you going?"

"I can't take these calls anymore. We're just wasting time. People are calling in and claiming most of the city could be the killer."

Sean agreed with Dave but that wasn't the point. On the off chance that they did get an important call, they needed as much manpower answering the phones as possible to take it. Sean pleaded with Dave. "We need you on the phone."

"You guys got the phones covered."

"What are you going to do then?"

Dave pointed at two boxes by their desks. They held personal items from the victims. "Have we checked their purses for receipts? Maybe they frequented the same places."

Sean hadn't done that yet, but he thought it was a good idea. He wanted to get off the phone just as much as Dave did, but he felt he had a responsibility not to. He nodded at Dave and conceded. "Ok. let me know what you find."

Carol called out over the bullpen, "I got another call."

Detective Hull shouted back, "Send it to me."

Sean watched Dave dig out the two purses until Carol called out again. This time he yelled back and took the call. He spoke to an older man on the phone in a nowhere conversation for a good five minutes before the call ended. He hung up the phone disappointed and thought about helping Dave, but Carol called out again. "Got another call."

Sean yelled back, "I'll take it."

He picked up the phone and Carol connected him. Sean began the conversation, "This is Detective Sean Kennedy with the Riverwood PD. How can I help you?"

The man on the other end of the line excitedly replied, "Hello, yes, my fourteen-year-old son told me that he saw something suspicious."

Sean sighed. It was another paranoid caller ringing in about his neighbor. The man continued. "He said he saw a very suspicious man walking in the park."

"The park?"

"Yes, the park."

Sean bit his lip. This man was wasting his time. He kept the conversation going and did his due diligence. "When did your son see this man?"

"Two nights ago. The night of that murder. He was walking home late on the ditch trail and said he saw a guy that just didn't feel right."

Sean heard the word ditch trail and his mind went back to the shadowed figure in the snow. He suddenly thought he might not be on a wasted call. This could be the witness he was waiting for. Sean asked the man. "What exactly was it that made your son suspicious? A lot of people walk on those trails."

"He said the man was acting as if he didn't want to be seen but when he saw my son, he hid something."

"What time was this at?"

Sean could hear the man talking to his son on the other line. He responded, "Around eight."

The timing was right too. Sean decided he needed a description. "Did your son describe what he looked like? It can be general, height, weight, age."

"He said he was average height, Caucasian, stockier build and anywhere from eighteen to thirty."

"Could your son identify the man if he ever saw him again?"

There was a pause over the line before the man replied, "He says he doesn't know. It was pretty dark out."

Sean's heart dropped. The kid wasn't even able to give them a hair color. He thanked the man for the call and hung up the phone. Sean was shaking his head at his desk when Dave called his name.

He turned and faced him. "I think I got something."

Sean got up from his desk and walked over. Dave held up two receipts and said, "Both of these receipts are for an oil change at Fenders Auto Body."

Sean didn't know if he should be surprised or not. The two victims did live close to each other and the chances were high that they went to the same places. Dave held them up for Sean to see and noted, "Abigail went in early January and Kathrine went a month ago."

Sean grabbed the two receipts. Dave was right.

Carol shouted out about another call. Sean and Dave heard Vincinni yell back from the bullpen, "Send it to me."

Sean looked back at Dave. "This is something."

"I think we should go check it out. Ask a few questions and if nothing pans out, we can come back to the phone calls."

Sean hated the idea of more phone calls and this was an honest excuse to get away from the desk. He could hear Vincinni painfully working through his conversation with what sounded like an elderly woman and nodded back to Dave, "Let's get out of here."

Chapter 6

Jake opened the door to the case room and flipped on the fluorescent lighting. He knew that the process he was about to begin could be painstaking, but he wanted to do it right. He walked down the row of file cabinets and stopped at the last one reading 1969. He slowly pulled open the drawer so its slides wouldn't stick to the track. A man of his word, Jake literally started with the first file in the drawer. The file read, *Bob Connelly Homicide Jan 8, 1969*. He thumbed for the next file that read, *Lynn Cook Homicide Jan 24, 1969*. He grabbed the two files and took them out of the case room and over to the small table outside, where Spears was already propped up with his coffee.

Jake took a seat and opened the first file. He read through the case summary as he had become accustomed to, scanning the words and trying to find anything that piqued his interest. *Victim is a middle-aged male.* Jake read on about a strangled body police had come across outside of a popular bar in the early morning. He flipped to the back of the file and found that the only things left in evidence were the officers' statements and the man's wallet.

Captain Spears interrupted Jake's train of thought. "Well, what do we have?"

Jake looked over at the case room. His plan was to go through every file until he found one that they could test for DNA evidence. He knew it was going to take a long time, but he wondered if there was a faster way. He looked back over at Spears and said, "The case is a dud. Nothing was left behind for us."

Spears could tell that Jake was cooking up something and he was curious how the kid was going to go on with this. He understood how painstaking reviewing every file would be and he wondered if Jake was having second thoughts. Spears asked, "What are you thinking?"

Jake rubbed his forehead just above his eyebrows. He wanted to go about the cases right, but he also wanted to find a better way to screen through them. He replied to Spears, "This is going to take too long."

The captain laughed at him, "Uh-huh, why do you think I brought the coffee?"

"What if I pull a bunch of files and start looking for what they have kept in evidence instead of looking at the case itself? That way we can organize them by cases that have a chance to be tested for DNA."

Spears didn't like the idea of a workaround. There wasn't a fast track to reviewing cold cases, but he figured he'd let the young detective work out his plan. He gave Jake a nod.

Jake got up from the table and went back for the file cabinet. Spears stayed behind with his arms folded, interested in how Jake planned on organizing the cases. He could hear Jake rummaging through the file cabinet before he stepped back out of the room with a handful of files. He set half of them down in front of Spears and half down in front of himself. Jake suggested, "Ok. let's just flip to the evidence logs and see what they got in storage."

Spears still hadn't unfolded his arms. His stern expression grew deeper as he asked, "What exactly are we looking for in the evidence logs?"

"Evidence from intimate murders, right? A sexual assault or a violent murder where the offender could have left DNA."

Still unsure of Jake's methods, Spears unfolded his arms and opened his first file. The pair sat in silence, reading over the old reports. Jake flipped through files front to back and made a lot of noise as he did it. Spears felt distracted by the commotion and stopped him. "This isn't going to work."

"What do you mean?"

"We're going to have to find out if these were violent

murders before we check to see if they have the evidence
we need to move forward."

Jake exhaled and nodded.

"We're going to have to read the summary first.
There's no workaround. That doesn't mean we have to
read everything in the report. We can scan them, but we
at least have to determine the method of the murder
before we can look for the evidence. We're doing this
backward."

Jake nodded again.

Spears restacked his files and asked, "So how do you
want to organize these?"

"I want to make separate piles with the cases. Ones
that may have the evidence we need and ones that clearly
don't. An 'Intimate Murder,' or 'Sexual Assault' pile and
an 'Other' pile."

Spears agreed. He knew this was how they had to
go about it, but he'd wanted Jake to come to that
realization. The captain understood that there was only
one way to go over cold cases, the painstaking and long,
but *correct*, way. He looked back at Jake and replied,
"Let's get to it."

The pair started fresh with their pile of cold cases.
One by one, they began to separate the cases into their
categories. Jake was moving through his files quickly but
paused and took a bit longer with one case. He flipped
wildly from the summary, through the photos, and to the

evidence log. Excited, Jake said, "I think I got one."

He continued reading the summary and flipping back to the evidence log before he said, "Yeah I got a murder and sexual assault case here. They still have the victim's shirt in storage."

Jake's eyes said it all, but Spears remained silent. He sipped his coffee and thought about the circumstances. Jake continued on optimistically, "That shirt is the key. It could have blood, hair or semen from the killer."

Spears wasn't as hopeful. He tried to slow Jake down by shaking his head and saying, "Let's think about it before we get ahead of ourselves. All they have is the shirt?"

Jake nodded.

"We can't use it. Remember, we didn't start using rape kits until the late 70s, so we don't have a for sure sample from the assault. If we did find semen on that shirt, who's to say it occurred with the homicide? What if it happened beforehand, consensually? Any blood or hair we find may have come from anyone, after the assault or before."

Jake's smile faded away. Spears took a sip of coffee and continued. "One of the hardest parts in collecting DNA samples is proving that they belong to our offender. We need to be sure that what we test belongs to the killer. That's the first issue we'll have to work through in order to keep the DA happy and actually get something done."

Jake nodded but he didn't fully understand. He thought the case he was looking at was straight forward, but Spears was saying that they needed more. The captain reached over and grabbed the file to look it over. He talked as he glanced at it, "Say a police officer had a bloody nose or someone couldn't stomach the crime scene and somehow got their DNA on the evidence. We have no way of knowing. There's a chance that the shirt does have the DNA we want, but since we don't have a rape kit to give us a solid deposit from the offender, we can't confidently test it for a DNA profile. We need to have a logical road map that can spell out what belongs to who and how."

Jake was overwhelmed. How would he be able to prove all of that? Spears set down his coffee and said, "This guy out in California. They claimed that he had dozens of assaults and multiple murders. They had to have confirmed his DNA before they put it into CODIS."

Jake nodded in agreement and Spears continued. "The California investigators had the good fortune of evidence overkill. With the case you just pulled, all we have is a lone shirt. We're missing redundancy. For that case, we would need another article of clothing or another victim's article of clothing. Basically, anything else that could physically tie the offender's DNA to another aspect of the case or a related one. We can't leave any room for another narrative."

Now Jake understood. Spears explained it well. Without redundancy in the evidence, they had nothing to prove. Jake asked, "So how do we find cases with redundancy?"

"The case you pulled would've worked if we had something else left behind, but we don't. The most concrete example I can think of are cases like the one in California. Cases that have repeat offenders leaving behind multiple deposits of DNA."

"How would we find a case like that?"

Spears put his hands together. "*Modus operandi.* We'd have to find cases involving the same methods, often against similar victims and sharing the same motive."

It was a lot to take in for Jake and it sounded like a lot of work. He took a deep breath and exhaled. Spears smiled, "Like I said. It's not going to be easy."

"Has Riverwood even had repeat offenders? I mean, I know in school they said they were more common than you think, but someone like a serial killer? In *Riverwood*?"

"Technically, a serial killer is someone who has killed more than two people. I know some of the cold cases here, but I don't know all of them. I'm sure we've had our fair share of crazies. Riverwood has been a city since 1969. That's almost fifty years. I wouldn't rule it out. We've had repeat rapists, burglars and crime families, I'm sure we've had repeat killers."

Spears jiggled his empty cup of coffee and got up

from the table. As he stood, he said, "I think you got a good hold of this. I'm going to go upstairs, refill my coffee and catch up on emails. If you find a pattern, follow it. If it makes sense to you, come and get me and we'll look into it together."

Spears pushed in his chair and headed up the stairs. Jake was left sitting at the table and staring at the cases in front of him. He felt a little intimidated by the work that lay ahead. Tracking cases by M.O. meant that he needed another pile to organize them by. He would still have to start by sorting them between a pile of intimate murders and sexual assaults or other cases. After that, he'd have to try to weed out cases with similarities.

Jake grabbed the files Spears had left on his side of the table and added them to his own pile. He planned on starting over again. He found a pen and paper so he could keep his thoughts straight and grabbed the first file, the case of the man strangled outside of the bar. Scanning through the file once more, he concluded the same thing he had before, it was a dud. He closed the file and moved it to the "other" pile before grabbing his second file. It read *Lynn Cook Homicide Jan 24, 1969*. He scanned through the summary. *Known prostitute found dead and naked in Addenbrooke Park*. He read on to the method of the murder. *Victim was stabbed to death*. He flipped to the evidence log, hoping they had some clothes, a blanket or shoes. All they had listed in storage was a knife found nearby, a shoe print and a whiskey bottle. Jake thought the file would have had a good chance if it had more evidence. The murder was intimate enough for the killer's DNA to be at the scene, but they didn't have enough to test in storage. He closed the file and placed it in the "other" pile.

He moved on to the next file from the stack. It read, *Abigail Thompson Homicide February 5, 1969.* Jake quickly scanned through the summary. *Middle-aged woman shot in her garage.* After reading the word "shot" and finding no mention of a sexual assault, he closed the file. It didn't happen close enough for a struggle and the killer's DNA wouldn't be there. He moved the case to the "other" pile and grabbed another case.

Jake continued with the process and was moving smoothly through the files. In no time he had gone through eight cases and already found two that potentially held sufficient evidence if they could be paired with another case. One was of a body brutally beaten and found in the back of an abandoned car and the other was the sexual assault he had gotten excited about earlier.

Jake reached back for his pile of files and pulled the ninth cold case from 1969. It read, *Katherine Sandoval Homicide April 7, 1969.* Jake scanned through the summary and something caught his eye. *Young adult woman found by her husband, stabbed to death in her garage while he was away.* It was the word "garage." He had just seen a murder in a garage five cases before, but this one was different. The killer had used a knife, not a gun.

Intrigued, he thought about the two cases. Spears had mentioned that repeat offenders would use the same methods in carrying out their crimes. These two cases didn't have the same method from a first glance, but the victim was similar. In both cases, it was a lone female. Jake read on about the stabbing. *The garage side door had been broken into and the overhead garage light was removed in what appears to be a way to disorient the victim.*

Jake began to feel excited. If the overhead light was in fact removed by the killer, then the murder was premeditated. That meant they had a killer planning his act. Which also meant there was a chance the killer had done something like this before.

Jake looked through his other pile until he found the garage shooting from February. He opened the Abigail Thompson file and scanned it back through the summary. *Assailant broke into the garage by smashing the side door window to unlock the door.* Jake's excitement grew. His eyes raced faster across the poor, dated handwriting until he found it. *The overhead garage light was missing.* The sentence sent a chill down his spine and set his heart racing. He couldn't believe it. He read the words again to make sure he hadn't misread them.

He picked up his pen and began to list the similarities between the two cases. He read on, looking for more confirmation that the crimes were related. *No appearance of a sexual assault.* He flipped over to the Sandoval knife murder. *Does not look as though the victim was assaulted.* "Holy shit," Jake said to himself. No matter how he looked at the evidence he had two related murders.

Jake turned the Sandoval case back over to the end of the summary and continued reading. The detectives had to see the correlation between the murders. They were only months apart. Sure enough, hidden in the final thoughts of the lead detective and written near the end of the report was the confirmation Jake was looking for. *Similar to the Thompson case from February.*

He flipped back to the front of the file to look for the detectives on the case. There he found the names Bobby Hull, Steve Vincinni, David Maxwell and Sean Kennedy. Jake turned back over to the Thompson murder from February and found Sean Kennedy and David Maxwell.

Jake moved his two garage murders over to the side. He hoped, since he'd found two cases, he might find a third. He scanned through his remaining pile of cases. Looking for files with the detectives Kennedy and Maxwell on them. He pulled out one with their names on it and scanned it.

The file read, *Eugene Dole Homicide May 3, 1969.* The

case was of a cab driver found dead from a bullet in his back and left in an old parking lot. He pushed the file to the side and grabbed the next one.

This file read, *Helen Phillips Homicide May 29, 1969*. It was the type of file Jake was looking for. He had higher hopes being that the victim was a woman. He opened the case and started scanning the summary. Within seconds of his eyes hitting the first page, his heart rate began to race again. *Woman found stabbed to death in her garage.* Another garage murder. Jake didn't need any more reassurance. He knew he had found what he was looking for. He grabbed his notes and read back what he had jotted down between the other two cases.

- *Garage*
- *Broken side door*
- *Missing light*
- *Alone, young to middle-aged woman*
- *No sexual assault*

He checked off his garage note and read on. *Assailant broke into the side garage door.* He checked off the side door and his excitement built. His eyes wanted to move faster than he could read.

The light in the garage had been removed. Jake put another check. *Victim is a forty-two-year-old female.* He scribbled another check.

He wanted to spring out of his chair and run up to Spears, but he couldn't take his eyes off of the case. He read on until he found his last note. *No appearance of a sexual motive.* Jake dropped his pencil. He had found his repeat offender.

Chapter 7

1969

At five before nine on a Thursday night, May 29, 1969, Helen Phillips was lost in the pages of another book. She read everything she could find in the horror and science fiction genre. Ever since she watched her first Twilight Zone, she'd been hooked. She was usually caught up reading Isaac Asimov, H.G. Wells, Ray Bradbury or throwbacks from Edgar Allen Poe. Helen's favorite authors gave her the adventure of other worlds to escape to. The horror in their work captivated her imagination and always kept her turning the pages.

Reading was a hobby she adopted shortly after her husband succumbed to cancer. Since then, she'd lived her life as an after-work shut-in, hiding from the pain of her memories and repressing them with the written words of others.

Every night, Helen's house sat still like a quiet theater for her mind to play out the stories in her books.

The only light she kept was the lamp next to a couch she'd worn a distinct groove in over the years. Her nightly routine had become habitual and reliably predictable. Throughout her house, she'd left keepsakes from her husband. Household items that made it seem as though he wasn't gone. Her favorite and most visited was his beer fridge in the garage. She kept it stocked with his favorite three-two beer, the way he always did. She usually grabbed a couple as she read on, using the disorienting power of alcohol to climb deeper into her stories before they lulled her to sleep.

Tonight, she was turning the pages to Ray Bradbury's newest collection of short stories, *I Sing the Body Electric.* She had just finished the fourth story, *The Woman,* when she decided it was time for a beer. She dog eared her page and set it on the couch.

Walking swiftly through her dark house, Helen moved with purpose as though she would miss the next act. She quickly approached the door to the garage, but her storied brain stopped her. This was something she had been doing nightly for years but an article she had read in the paper during her break at work recently made her beer runs feel exciting. The article was the ongoing story of the Riverwood Garage Killer. Everyone in town had read about the murders in the paper and it was well known that garages had now overtaken basements as the most feared locations in Riverwood homes.

For Helen, the thrill of fear was something she sought from her books nightly. The story of the Garage Killer felt as though Bradbury had put her town in one of his books. Her experiences with fear were guided by what her mind imagined from the pages she read. It never felt real. The stories never seemed possible. The Garage Killer made her feel somewhere in between. She stood staring blindly at the cracks in the door while her mind wandered. It took her to a story she had read that stuck with her. A creepy, haunting, older story called *The Tell-Tale Heart,* one of Poe's most thrilling works.

She imagined the man, the servant, or simply the unknown murderous narrator from the story, standing behind her door. An individual who watched and obsessed over an old man until the compulsion to kill overcame his sanity of peace. The servant contently hid the old man's body under his room until the sound of his beating heart under the floorboards drove him mad.

Helen put her ear to the door, listening for a breathing servant, the sound of someone obsessed and driven to kill. She heard nothing.

The stories in her head mixed together. She now thought back to the one she just finished, *The Woman,* where a husband is drawn to an ocean that calls to him. An evil lurking presence exists in the water and wants to tempt him deeper and deeper until it has him.

Now, this was her garage, calling her in for her

nightly beer. Her ode to her late husband and the companion to her literary vice. She felt stiff and anxious standing in front of the door, knowing the dark room beyond it contained the possibility of something sinister. The papers told her so.

Recognizing the feeling of fear, Helen began to embrace it as she always had, constantly turning the pages to hold onto the thrill. Reading on to get lost in the story. Intuition took hold of her. She grabbed the knob, twisted it over and turned the page.

Helen held the door open. Peering into the garage, the small light from her living room lamp barely illuminated the darkness in front of her. Her heart was beating faster from the anxiety she'd worked up before opening the door.

She stepped into the cold room and let the door close behind her. She felt she needed heightened senses and was listening beyond her breath for anything out of the ordinary. Helen knew the way in the dark. She never parked her car in the garage and knew that there was nothing in front of her to bump into. She always tended to rush through the scary parts of her stories. The anticipation of the moment made her too eager to know what would happen next. Now she was rushing through her garage.

Never needing the overhead light, she masterfully made her way to the fridge and placed her hand on the door. She pulled it open, illuminating the room with a faint beige glow. The light acted as a lantern, only allowing her to see three feet beyond where she stood.

Helen bent over, grabbed her beer and stood up. She let go of the fridge, making the weight of the door close itself, and turned back towards her house. The dim light quickly faded and her eyes adjusted to the darker environment, allowing her to see deeper into the garage.

Just as the door back into her home withdrew from view and before the light fully disappeared in the garage, Helen's heart jumped into her throat. Standing on the other end of the room was the silhouette she had read about on her breaks at work.

Motionless. Void of definition. The man was watching her. She held her breath and the door to the fridge closed with a bang, leaving her in the blacked-out garage with the man.

Now she was the old man in Poe's story. Now she had the final piece to understand her favorite narrative. She was the character on the other side. The one in the room. Her heart wasn't beating through the floorboards but through her chest.

~ ~ ~

Sean and Dave had gone through a rough month. They were, once again, sitting well outside a reasonable timeframe to feel hopeful about the case of Kathrine Sandoval or the related case of Abigail Thompson. Their drive to check out Fenders Auto Body had turned into a waste of time. The owner refused to allow them to see any of his employees, fearing they would be harassed. He claimed he didn't know the women, and that he had seen the stories in the paper, but he couldn't connect either of them with any of his workers. He acknowledged that the victims had their cars serviced in his shop, but he didn't have anything else for the detectives. Sean and Dave left the autobody disappointed. All they could do was return to the phones.

In the time being, they were assigned another dud of a case. It briefly stole their attention and served as a distraction from the garage murders they found more compelling. No matter how many weeks passed, Sean and Dave couldn't keep their minds off of the Garage Killer. The detectives still couldn't settle on a motive and their greatest fear was receiving a call in the night to another lonely home.

They both felt that since there had been two murders, they could expect a third. They loathed the idea of reliving the frustrations they had already been through twice, but it only seemed like a matter of time. Hearing the phone ring at the station and listening to the buzz of the radio made them anxious. They could tell that the case was weighing on them, making them paranoid. However, time brought them no relief and in the early morning hours of May 30, their fears were realized.

Sean stepped out of Dave's patrol car in front of 3478 Herman Street. A coworker of Helen Philips had called the police about her absence at work. Soon after, a patrolman found her broken garage door and let himself inside.

Detectives Hull and Vincinni met Sean and Dave at the house. Christopher and his team weren't far behind. The detectives made it inside the garage and carefully gathered around the crime scene. Everyone there seemed to be a bit on edge. At this point, the murders were beginning to feel personal. They knew the whole city would be reading the story in the next day's paper and that they were the ones who were going to have to speak for it.

Sean took a look at the body. It was fully clothed and covered in blood and stab wounds. Like the two times before, he could see the garage light was missing. He let out a sigh and said what everyone in the room already knew. "We got another one."

He bent down next to the body and inspected the victim's hand as he'd seen Christopher do. He couldn't see anything under her fingernails. The group could hear the sound of the forensics team showing up. Christopher walked through the broken door and stared around the garage. His team followed behind and ventured into the house. Dave spoke to Christopher as he walked in. "It's just like the last one. No light, side door, stabbed and clothes on."

Sean began to walk out of the room and gestured the

other detectives to follow. He patted Christopher on the shoulder as he moved passed him, "We'll leave you to it. We're going to hit some doors. We'll pay you another visit tonight." Christopher nodded and the detectives filed out of the garage.

In the yard outside of the house, Sean spoke to the group. "Same as last time. You guys go left, we'll go right. Most people are at work, so I'm not expecting a lot of answers."

"I'm not either," said Vincinni as he shook his head, "No one called us last night. Even if we do get an answer at the door, I don't think the neighbors know anything."

They all agreed with Vincinni but spread out to knock on doors anyway. They had just arrived at the crime scene but already, the group felt pessimistic. It was going to be another long twenty-four hours.

As the detectives had assumed, the neighbors were clueless about the crime. The killer had successfully kept another murder quiet. Sean and the other detectives returned to the station to prepare for the press conference. He remembered how tough the last one had been and was worried that this one was going to go the same.

When Sean and Dave entered the small conference room it was already filled with the usual crowd. They took a seat and watched Chief Perry set the stage. He gave his normal report, detailing the known highlights of the murder, the facts that undoubtedly linked the case to the previous two.

By the time Chief Perry was finished, the energy in the room was tangible. Each reporter wore a concerned face. The chief answered only a few questions, leaving the room hungry for more. He once again looked to Sean to handle the rest of the Q&A.

Sean nervously got up from his seat and walked over to the temporary podium in the front of the room. He didn't even bother to gloss over another summary of the case. He'd learned his lesson the first time. Looking beyond the crowd to avoid direct eye contact, he addressed the reporters and acted in his best attempt at confidence, saying, "I'll take your questions when you're ready."

His words were like flicking a switch. Every hand in the room shot up.

Sean began picking them one by one.

"Nathan Retti, *The Denver Post*. Detective, are you looking into all of these garage murders as congruent cases or copycats? It sounds like it's safe to assume this is all the work of one man."

Sean exhaled and braced for a long Q&A. "We are looking into all of them as linked cases, yes."

Eyes darted down to notepads before eagerly returning to Sean. He pointed at another.

"Ed Donaldson, *Rocky Mountain News*." Sean clenched

his hands. He never read Ed's piece the last time around, but he had heard from enough concerned citizens because of it. He was anxious about what other panic Ed would cause with his next article. Ed continued on, "Since we now know that this is the third murder of the Garage Killer, what precautions will you take going forward, and what's your message to the people of Riverwood?"

Sean immediately hated the question but tried hard not to show it. He responded calmly, "We are going to increase our night patrols, as well as rely on the strong community bonds here in Riverwood to hopefully help report any suspicious activity. What we ask of the city is that people look out for their neighbors. The last thing we want is for there to be another murder. We want to assure the city we are working diligently, around the clock, on this case."

He quickly moved on from Ed, trying to avoid a follow-up question, and pointed at another.

"Ken Poland, *Riverwood Sentinel.* It's been three months since the first garage murder. Do we have any suspects?"

It was a fair question, but it stung. Sean wanted to keep his answers as vague as possible to avoid speculation. He didn't care what the papers said about him the next day, but he didn't want to put a bad name on his station. He replied, "We are reviewing persons of interest, but I ask your readers to please call in if they have any information regarding the case."

The reporters knew what that meant. The case was still wide open. Sean continued answering questions until the press conference ended in the afternoon. The only thing they could hope for was a slightly positive read in the paper. As much as they hated sitting through the phone calls that came after the stories were printed, they knew there was always a chance a legitimate call could come in.

Dave caught Sean on their way out of the conference room and said, "Christopher and Mark have had enough time. Let's get over there."

Sean was tired and wanted a break, but he knew they couldn't afford it. He nodded back at Dave and they went on their way.

The detectives parked their car in front of the county buildings. It had already been a tough day and it was only halfway through. Dave rubbed his hand over his forehead and said, "Let's make this as quick as possible."

They got out of the car and headed into the Coroner's office. They walked the familiar route to where they knew they could find Mark and opened the double doors. Mark greeted the detectives as he saw them. "Gentlemen, welcome back."

He handed them the file he had put together and

began to recite it. Sean pulled out a notebook and stepped near the body as Mark began. "I hate to sound like a broken record, but this is just like the last one. We have seventeen stab wounds. Our victim was not sexually assaulted, and it appears the killer used the same or a similar knife. We have no apparent sign of her fighting back. Her hands aren't bruised, and her fingernails are clean. I noted the time of death as around 9 p.m. to 10 p.m. We only recovered her blood type, which was B positive."

Sean wrote everything down and looked up at Mark. "Is that it?"

"That's everything."

Sean closed his notebook and thanked him. The detectives took one last look at the body of Helen Philips before leaving Mark and walking away.

Next door, at the crime lab, they hoped for a better outcome. They found Christopher in his desk and sat down in the corduroy chairs they'd become familiar with over the past few months. Dave started the conversation, "How's it going, Christopher? Did we give you enough time?"

"We've had the time; we just don't have the evidence."

Sean and Dave knew he didn't have much to work with. Christopher continued, "No luck on the prints and we really couldn't find anything else in the house. We did, however, find a footprint outside. A men's size ten. It was in the dirt under the living room window."

Sean replied, "Size ten? That was one of the sizes you guys found outside of the Sandoval house as well, right?"

Christopher nodded. Sean and Dave knew they couldn't do anything with it, but it was still interesting information. Christopher sighed, "That's all I have on this one. Have you guys seen Mark?"

The detectives nodded.

"Anything I need to know?"

They both shook their heads.

The group sat in silence, each waiting for the other to bring up an interesting piece about the case, but nothing came to mind. They all knew that they needed more information and they didn't have it. Sean eventually got up and nudged Dave to follow, speaking to Christopher as they stood, "Thanks, Christopher. We'll let you know if we have any updates."

Disheartened, the detectives headed back for the station.

On their way back, Sean and Dave drove past Helen Philip's house. They knocked on two extra doors now that more of the neighbors were home, but they still didn't have any luck on finding a witness. They left the neighborhood and returned to the station in silence.

As they walked through the front door, Carol called out to them, "I have a message for you two."

"Who's it from?" Sean asked as he made it over to her.

Carol dug around in the notes she had at her desk. "It's from a man at Fenders Auto Body. He said he was the owner. A man named Jack Barlow."

Sean looked over at Dave. They were surprised to hear from him again. Sean replied to Carol, "What did he want?"

"He just asked for a callback. I put his number and a note on your desk."

Sean thanked Carol and walked back to the bullpen. There he found the note she had written to him. Dave was standing over his shoulder and said, "Let's call him."

They both took a seat and Sean picked up the phone. He dialed the number and put the receiver to his ear. It rang twice before the call connected.

"Hello, this is Jack."

Sean assumed it was his home number and replied, "Hello Jack. This is Detective Sean Kennedy. You called?"

Sean could hear the man sigh on the other line. "Yeah. Ever since you paid me a visit, I've been keeping an eye out on the guys. I heard about what happened."

"Yeah, we've had another one."

"I didn't think much of it before, but I have an

employee who is giving me some reasons for concern."

"What exactly is it that this employee has done?"

Jack sighed again, "I may just be acting paranoid, but this guy is saying some real weird stuff about women. He's been flaky at work lately and oddly aggressive."

"Would you mind sharing his name?"

There was a pause over the line until Jack said, "Daryl Welch."

Sean wrote the name down and slid it over to Dave. He replied, "I appreciate your concern, Mr. Barlow. Is there any way you could come down to the station so we could talk more?"

"Yeah, yeah I can do that."

"How's tomorrow at nine in the morning sound?"

Jack grumbled back, "Saturday?"

"Yeah, Saturday."

Jack eventually agreed and hung up the phone. Sean looked back over at Dave and said, "Well, that was interesting."

"He suspicious of this Daryl Welch huh?"

"I guess. We'll have him in tomorrow. Have we checked if Helen Philips went to that auto body?"

Dave shook his head, "No, but we have her things right here."

Dave walked over and grabbed Helen's purse out of a box of her belongings. He opened it up and looked inside. "I don't see any receipts in here."

He handed the purse over to Sean, who grabbed the purse and quickly checked it. He couldn't find any receipts either and said, "We can try to ask Jack about her tomorrow. I'm sure they keep records."

Dave put Helen's purse back. It was nearing the end of the day for the detectives and their lack of a break had caught up to them. Dave looked over at the clock and said, "I'm going to go home and get some sleep. We have the auto body guy coming at nine?"

Sean nodded.

Dave gathered his things and got up from his desk. He patted Sean on the shoulder as he walked past him. "Go home. Try to sleep. You'll burn yourself out if you stay too much longer."

Sean watched Dave leave and stayed at his desk. He knew he wouldn't be able to sleep when he went home anyway, but eventually, he packed up his notes and left the station.

Later that night Sean tossed and turned in his bed. His troubled mind couldn't turn off. He spent a few hours trying to get to sleep but it was pointless. Around midnight he forced himself up, careful not to wake his wife, Judy. He walked out of his house and sat in his car.

He knew why he couldn't sleep. It was the snowy figure from February. He tortured himself with the idea that the man would return. He still hadn't told Dave about that night, but out of everything in the case, it was what troubled him the most. It made him feel like the killer was rubbing it in. He grabbed his pistol, put it on his lap and backed the car out of the driveway.

When Sean turned on Helen's street, he killed the lights and rolled to a stop outside of 3478 Herman. This time he turned off the radio. He lit a cigarette and stared at the house. His eyes made jumpy moves up and down the street, scanning the shadows for anything that moved.

He finished his cigarette and his awareness began to fade. He needed to stay awake, but his eyes were growing heavy. He put his head against his driver's seat and stared at the streetlight a few houses away when something caught his eye.

He perked up and stared at it. It was a house cat, lazily crossing the street. Sean took a deep breath and sunk back down. The cat made him feel like a fool. He was jumpy and tired. After a few minutes, his eyes grew heavy again. He could feel himself waning and eventually gave in.

When he opened his eyes, the sun was braking over the horizon. In a panic he looked around, briefly forgetting where he was until his memory came back to him. Realizing what had happened, Sean shook his head. He only had a couple of hours before Jack from Fenders Auto Body would show up at the station. Sean turned on his car and headed over.

Sean walked into the station a mess. The reporters' questions the day before still rang in his head. He was worried that they doubted him and his team. They needed something conclusive, a narrative that they could tie someone to. He was excited to speak with Jack from Fenders, but he wanted more. The adaptiveness of the man they were after worried him. He was smart enough to switch from using a gun to a knife and Sean wondered what he would tweak next. He had no doubt in his mind that they would have another murder soon and he needed to put more pressure on the killer to flush him out.

Sean looked over at the clock. He still had two hours before Jack showed up and most likely an hour before Dave would come in. He walked over to the break room and poured himself a cup of coffee. He needed to shake off his tunnel vision and his sleepless night. Caffeine and cigarettes usually did the trick. He stepped outside the station into a fresh dawn and took in the spring morning. The scent of dew and cut grass revitalized him. The air was mixed with the billowing smell of bacon from the diner next door. Sean lit his cigarette and closed his eyes.

Alone and stimulated he could think. His train of thought led him to the only unique piece of evidence between the cases, the pistol. He knew he had no way of tracking a purchased pistol but there had to be something he could do with the information. He thought about trying to track stolen pistols but quickly dismissed the concept. Sean knew it would only lead him to more questions, but the idea got him in the right mindset.

Sean had been stuck thinking about what they didn't have and was paying no attention to what they did have. He smoked more of his cigarette and leaned into the idea. He realized they didn't have to always look into writing new paperwork when they could dig into old ones.

Christopher had told them that the pistol used was the same model given to military service members. If the killer acquired his pistol through the military, then they could work a whole new angle.

Sean assumed that his killer had a previous record. He reasoned that no ordinary man could possibly carry the skill set used in the garage murders without experience. As the murders stood, the detectives were without a suspect and the case was still wide open, but if Sean narrowed his focus to veterans with criminal records, then he had someplace to start.

The idea felt like a stretch, but it was more than what they currently had. If he was able to get a hold of the criminal records of Riverwood's veterans, then maybe he could build a potential suspect list. The new approach would let him identify people of interest whom they otherwise would have never looked into. He took one last drag of his cigarette, threw it down and went back into the station.

It was eight in the morning when Dave walked in. He wasn't surprised to find Sean already at his desk and said to him, "You look like shit. Did you sleep here?"

Sean waved him off and looked at the newspaper under his arm. He asked, "What the hell is that?"

"It's the *Rocky Mountain News*."

Sean gave Dave an unsettled look and Dave felt like he had to explain himself. "We need to know what they're saying about us."

Sean shook his head and looked at his desk. "How bad is it?"

"Not the best. Ed didn't hold anything back on this one."

"Well, what's it say?"

Dave put down his things and took a seat. He took a deep breath and filled Sean in. "For the second time, he has compared the acts of the Garage Killer to the Viet Cong. He even gave him a name."

Dave threw the paper in front of Sean. He couldn't help but read the title, "Garage Guerrilla Claims Another."

Sean closed his eyes and sighed. This wasn't going to go over easy with the city. He grabbed the paper and threw it back on Dave's desk saying, "I don't want to read it," and quickly changed the subject. "I thought of something this morning."

"What's that?"

"The gun. Christopher said a lot of veterans have them. What if we checked the criminal records of River-wood's veterans? Perhaps we'd find someone we otherwise wouldn't be looking for?"

"That's not a bad idea," replied Dave.

"We can ask Vincinni and Hull to look into it, too. I'm sure it could turn into a rabbit hole if we're not careful."

Dave nodded and looked at the clock. They needed to prepare for Jack. He changed the subject to the interview. "Are you ready for this guy?"

Sean replied, "Yeah, I'm ready for him. I figure he'll lead the conversation; we just have to steer him in the right direction and see what he's got."

Jack Barlow showed up early. He was a bit nervous and fidgety with his hands. The detectives led him to the conference room where they sat around a table. Dave grabbed him a cup of coffee and said, "Jack, thanks for coming down on your weekend. We were hoping we could talk to you about Daryl's day on Thursday. Was he at work that day?"

Jack was tense, he took small sips of his coffee and replied, "He was there. Worked until six."

Sean took his notepad out and let Dave do the talking. Dave asked, "Do you know what he did after work?"

"Unfortunately, no."

"What about during the day? Did he do anything unusual?"

Jack shook his head.

"What about Friday? The day you called us. What was it that made you call?"

Jack looked down and sighed, "He came in late that day and had an attitude. I heard about the murder that happened the night before from a couple of customers and the word spread around the shop. Daryl thought the whole thing was hilarious. He was talking about it like he was bragging about it. Saying how easy it is and how no one will ever catch the guy."

Dave responded, "Did he have that reaction to the last two murders?"

"All three."

Dave looked over at Sean and then said, "The woman that was killed on Thursday was named Helen Philips. Do you know if she got her car serviced at your shop?"

"I'm not sure but I can check."

"Your employee, Daryl, what does he look like?"

"He's got black hair, fair skin and is roughly five-foot-ten."

"Would you say he's stocky?"

Jack nodded. "Yeah, I'd say so."

"What about shoe size. Do you know what size shoes he has?"

"Um, I'm unsure. I'd say average."

"So, size ten maybe?"

"Sure."

Dave paused to let Sean catch up on his notes and asked, "Do you know his address?"

Jack nodded.

Dave gestured at Sean's notebook and Sean ripped out a page. "Could you write it down for us?"

He slid the ripped paper and pen over to Jack and said, "If we do find it necessary to speak to Daryl, we, of course, won't mention you."

Jack looked hesitant but wrote the address down. Dave smiled and said, "Thank you, Jack. Is there anything else you want to discuss with us?"

Jack stayed quiet and shook his head. Dave stood up and replied, "Well, sir, if that's it then thank you for your time."

Jack got up from the table and nodded at the detectives. He started for the door and turned back to say, "I'll let you know about that name."

Dave replied, "Yeah, Helen Philips. We'd appreciate it."

Jack walked himself out. Sean looked down at his notes and said, "Well, Daryl matches the vague description we have but so does half of Riverwood."

"I don't know. He had the intuition to come down here and talk to us. That's something."

"Yeah, I guess you're right. We can keep our eyes on Mr. Welch. Save his address for a rainy day."

Chapter 8

Spears was in his office. It had been two hours since he left Jake in the basement with the cold cases. He was still going through unanswered emails when a stack of files appeared next to him. He looked over to a grinning detective.

"I found one," said Jake as he pointed at the files.

Surprised, Spears replied, "Already?"

Jake nodded.

"Are you sure?"

"Yeah, I couldn't believe it either. These were all from 1969."

Spears looked over at the three files and picked the first one up. He read the summary of the Abigail Thompson case. After he finished, he picked up the Kathrine Sandoval case. As he read, he spoke to Jake. "All three of these are related?"

"They have to be."

Spears moved on to the Helen Philips case. His eyes quickly scanned the words and then widened. "Wow, you're right. These *must* be related." He finished reading and looked back at his young detective. "I'm amazed, Jake. Good job."

Jake reached in his pocket, unfolded the notes he had taken in the basement and said, "These are the similarities I found between the cases." He set the list in front of Spears. "I was looking for intimate murders like we talked about, and originally skipped over that first case, but after I found the second one, I pulled it back out."

Spears looked over the list and asked, "They all share these?"

"Yeah, the only difference between them is the murder weapon used in the first one."

Jake watched Spears look between the cases and asked, "In the back of the files the detectives even listed that the cases were similar. Why weren't they kept in the same file?"

"They were three separate homicides so they would each get their own file. I'm sure the original detectives had boxes of other files that went with these, but they most likely took them when they left or threw them in storage."

Spears flipped the files over to the evidence logs and said, "It looks like they have some things in the warehouse."

"Yeah, that's the best part. We still have the victims' clothing from the two knife cases. That should be all we need right?"

Spears looked up from the files. "Hopefully — and that's a big hope — but yeah, that's what we're after."

The captain got up from his desk and closed the files to say, "This is impressive, Jake. Let's go show these to the chief. He might know about these cases."

Jake followed Spears over to Kelly's office. Spears knocked on the door and Kelly greeted them as they both walked in. "Gentlemen, what can I do for you?"

Spears replied, "Chief, Jake found some interesting cases here from 1969. They all appear to be connected. Do you know about these?" Spears placed the files on his desk and took a seat.

Kelly slid the files over and opened the first one up. He glanced over the Abigail Thompson case and reminiscently smiled. Replying, "Yeah, I know about these. This guy was a big deal when I was a kid. He used to have a nickname, they called him the Garage Guerrilla."

Jake was now sitting in the chair next to Spears with growing excitement. Hearing that the killer he had just discovered had a pseudonym made him even more interested in the cases.

"The Garage Guerrilla?" asked Spears.

"That's what the papers called him. As you've probably read in the files, he attacked women in their garages at night. He would wait for them and take out the lights, so they were unable to see."

Spears had never heard of the killer before. He asked, "Did you ever look into these?"

"No, no they were already twenty-year-old cold cases by the time I came around. A few of the old-timers were still obsessed with them back then, but they never passed it down." Kelly smiled. "Yeah, this case brings back memories. I remember all the Colorado big ones: Bundy, The Bennet hammer murders, Thomas Luther. There seems to be one for every decade."

Spears brought the conversation back around to the cases in front of them and said, "There's nothing new in these files saying that anyone has ever approached modern DNA collection. Our goal, since Jake started a couple of weeks ago, was to bring a case forward to test at the lab. Is that something we can do?"

Kelly nodded. "I love that idea. I think it'd be great experience for Jake and if these cases never had it done before and still have something left behind to test, then even better. I can hold off Julie for a little bit longer and give you guys time to get something together." The chief put his hands together. "I sure would love to put this case through CODIS."

Without hesitation Jake replied, "Or that website."

Jake watched Kelly's expression to see what he thought of the idea. The chief didn't look opposed and he responded in confidence. "If the lab has the capability to do that and it doesn't cost an arm and a leg, then I see no harm in it. I know you're inspired to try it, Jake."

The response electrified the young detective. Just like that, they had the approval they needed.

Kelly looked down at the files before saying, "It's probably too late in the day for you guys to head over to the warehouse and start taking down boxes. I'd say your next step is getting all the information together. The guys who originally worked on these cases may still be around; you can try to give them a call, but I'd wait to do that until after you've fully familiarized yourselves with everything you can find."

Jake replied, "How do we find out more? It looks like all we have in storage is the evidence itself."

"You can always head over to the library next week and see what old newspapers you can pull up."

Satisfied, Spears got up from his chair and said, "Thanks chief, we'll let you know what progress we've made by the end of next week."

Jake got up and followed Spears out of the room. He walked over with him to his office, unsure of what to do next. He asked Spears, "Why can't we just pull up those old newspapers on the internet?"

Spears responded, "They most likely aren't on the internet. The Denver library keeps a lot of old newspapers in microfilm. They have machines you can use there called microfilm readers. We can go next week and check it out."

Jake was too excited. "I think I'll go this weekend."

Spears smiled at him. "It's your weekend. I'll catch up with you on Monday."

The next day, Saturday morning, Jake parked his car a couple of blocks from the Denver library. The morning sun was shining warmly, and the air smelled sweet with blooming cherry blossoms and freshly cut grass. Jake stepped into the building's lobby and walked over to an information desk. The man on the other side greeted him. "Hi, how can I help you?"

Jake looked around the large structure in awe and replied, "I'm looking for the microfilm machines."

The man pointed at a map on the wall and said, "Fifth floor. Western History."

Jake studied the map and then took to the stairs. He found his way to the fifth floor and walked up to the Western History desk. A woman behind the desk looked at him in acknowledgment. Jake pulled out a piece of paper on which he had written the dates of the homicides and said, "Hello, I was hoping to pull a few newspapers from 1969. *The Denver Post* and the *Rocky Mountain News.*"

"Which dates?"

"Early February, early April and late May."

"Ok. Why don't you find a machine and I'll bring those over for you."

Jake walked over to the large machines and sat down at one that was open. The machines looked like they belonged to another decade. They had large flat screens that resembled an old computer, with fat knobs and manual switches. Jake stared at them in bewilderment. A few minutes later the woman returned with small cases containing film. She looked at Jake and asked, "Do you know how to use these?"

Jake shook his head. She opened the cases and started to instruct him. "You insert the films like this." Jake watched her take the film out and put it on a spindle. "Keep the film on top and push it all the way in. Then you open the feeder and lock it in. After that, you hit this button, which grabs the film, and you're all set."

Jake thanked her and she walked away. She had uploaded the February edition of *The Denver Post*. The projected picture was grainy but clear enough to read. Jake scanned the film over to February 5, 1969, the date of Abigail Thompson's murder and quickly went through the pages but found nothing related to the homicide. He scrolled down and began to pore over the paper from the following day and again found nothing.

Moving onto two days from the murder, his eyes were attracted to the title of a side article on the front page, "Single Mother Murdered in Garage." Jake moved past the headline and scrolled to the story. There he found a lot of what he had read in the case report. The writer spoke of the murder's uncommon nature and blamed the busier population of Denver for the homicide, noting that it wasn't something a member of the Riverwood community was capable of.

Jake printed the article and attempted to follow the librarian's steps in reverse. He removed the film and loaded up the same timeframe of the *Rocky Mountain News*. Again, he scrolled down until two days after the murder and found a story titled, "Woman Murdered in Riverwood Home." This, too, wasn't headline-worthy. Another side article in a gloomy paper trying to paint the bright side of the times. The article carried a similar tone to the other paper. It was written as if the story was a rarity for the area. The author wrote dramatically, and his overly long article milked the situation for an attention grab.

Jake printed the article and removed the cartridge. He snagged the next *Rocky Mountain News* film and loaded it in. He scrolled to the date of the second murder, April 7, 1969. Jake scanned through the paper and went onto the following day. He stopped at the headline of the first page, "Garage Killer Strikes Again." This time, the dramatic author wrote a much longer article than he had on the first one. Jake skimmed the words. The writing no longer blamed the more crime-familiar Denver, as the two articles had before. It carried a more ominous tone and asked for the citizens of Riverwood to be watchful of others. Once more the author seemed to overdo it. Jake winced at his most emotional lines:

This killer has brought home the horrors of war that our boys face in the guerrilla fighting of the jungles abroad. He is a monster who stalks our streets, preys on our women and personifies our greatest fears. He has invaded our homes and stolen our sense of security. This Garage Guerrilla must be stopped.

There it was. Jake read how the killer got his name. The article was moving but at the time it must have caused quite the trouble. It undoubtedly gave the killer the attention he so desperately craved.

Jake printed the article and removed the film. Amused with the writer from the *Rocky Mountain News*, he grabbed the last film and loaded it in. He scrolled to the date of the third murder, May 29, 1969, and skimmed down until the next day's paper. There, as the Saturday headline, he found the article. It was titled, "Garage Guerrilla Claims Another." Jake read the most dramatic piece yet. The writer doubled down on his call for caution and warned the citizens of Riverwood to look amongst themselves. If the last article troubled the city, this one put it in a full-blown panic.

Jake printed the article and removed the film. He grabbed *The Denver Post* films containing the articles for the second and third murders and went on to print their versions of the murders as well. After he was done, he returned the films to the librarian.

Jake was happy he had come to see the articles, but he hadn't necessarily learned anything the case files hadn't already told him. However, he now understood how much attention the crime spree received at the time. He felt he had seen everything he could find about the cases and was eager to move on to the next step. He'd bring the printed articles to Spears come Monday and together, they'd attempt to track down the old detectives. Jake couldn't wait to hear what they had to say.

That Monday, Jake drove to the station with the printed news stories. He figured Spears would be pleased to know that he saved him a traffic-filled drive down to Denver. Jake arrived early and waited until the captain got settled at his desk before he walked over.

When Jake made it into his office, Spears was expecting him. The captain said, "Well, how'd it go?"

Jake set the printed articles on his desk and took a seat. "This is what I found. They don't tell us much that we don't already know, but they're entertaining."

Spears grabbed the articles and looked over them. He took his time jumping between the stories and replied, "Appears this guy got plenty of attention."

"The articles make the cases sound pretty high profile. I bet everyone around here back then knew about it."

Spears agreed. He put the printouts down and looked over at Jake. "If this is everything that we have, then I think we've seen enough. We don't have too much time so I'd like to try to move on and see if we can reach anyone from the original investigation team."

It was exactly what Jake wanted to hear. He had waited all weekend to find out who they could talk to. Spears reached over and grabbed the Abigail Thompson file. Jake watched the captain open the file and look at the detectives on the case, asking, "Do we have their numbers saved somewhere?"

"I doubt it," said Spears. "These guys left a long time ago."

Spears reached down under his desk and opened a cabinet. He dug his hand inside and pulled out a large phone book. He dropped it on the table and said, "This is from 2012 but if these guys are still around, I bet they'll be at the same places." He shoved it over to Jake. "Have you ever used one of these before?"

"The white pages? Not in a while but yeah, I remember how. It's just alphabetical right?"

Spears nodded and looked back at the cold case file. "Ok. See if you can find a David Maxwell."

Jake opened the book and flipped the pages over to the M's. He found the right page and started scanning the names, speaking as he read. "There's an Adam Maxwell and a Daniel. Here, I got him. Dave and Cindy Maxwell. They have an address in Riverwood."

Spears grabbed his desk phone. "What's the number?"

Jake looked down at the page and read it off. Spears dialed the number and put the phone on Speaker. It rang three times, then they heard a loud rustling on the other end as someone answered.

"Hello?"

The voice of a younger woman came over the line.

Spears responded to her, "Yes, I'm looking for David Maxwell."

A brief pause came over the phone before the woman's voice came back. "Oh, I'm sorry sir, but Mr. Maxwell passed away three years ago."

Spears had worried that would be the case. He thanked the woman and hung up.

Jake shook his head and said, "Shit, I hope we still have the other guy."

Spears looked back at the file and read the other name out to Jake. "Look up Sean Kennedy."

Jake turned the pages over to the K's and quickly read through the names. He called out, "Here he is. Sean and Judy Kennedy."

Jake read the number out to Spears. He dialed the number and put the phone back on speaker. The phone rang twice and then connected. This time an older man's voice came from the other side.

"Hello."

Spears replied, "Hello sir. I'm looking for Sean Kennedy."

The old man responded, "May I ask who's calling?"

"This is Captain Alonzo Spears with the Riverwood Police."

Two long seconds passed. Spears began to think the man didn't hear him and was about to speak again when the voice came back.

"Well captain, you're talking to him."

Chapter 9

It was Wednesday night, six days after the murder of Helen Philips. The release of the *Rocky Mountain News* on Saturday buried the detectives in a wave of never-ending calls. All Sean and Dave had been able to do was sift through the noise and listen to concerned citizens and a frenzied public.

Dave was slouched in his chair, his hand on his forehead, trying to fight a pounding headache. Sean was next to him at his desk over a pile of criminal records, desperately trying to find a lead. The detectives thought they were going mad.

They had received a call from Jack Barlow from Fenders Auto Body telling them that Helen Philips had not been a customer, but they were still interested in his employee, Daryl Welch. The detectives wanted to knock on his door, but they didn't feel they had enough reason. Besides the receipts Dave had found, they had nothing that tied him to the three murders. All that they had on him was hearsay from his boss.

As it was, they were receiving calls from the community reporting suspicious neighbors daily, and they didn't have the time to investigate each one. They would need more evidence before they confronted anyone. Sean and Dave both agreed that if Welch was their man, then knocking on his door would only give him the upper hand. Without the ability to hold him they would inadvertently give him the time to clean up his tracks and close off loose ends. All they could do was keep an eye on him.

Sean had asked Hull and Vincinni to help with going through the criminal records of Riverwood's veterans. The task required reviewing every record they could find from veterans who served in World War Two up until the ongoing war in Vietnam. Through the criminal records, the team hoped to build a list of persons of interest. GI's who had been convicted of violent crimes and break-ins. Yet, even with the names they gained from the records, the same rules applied as to how they were handling Welch. The detectives would be forced to wait until they had more.

Dave was hitting his breaking point for the day and sat up in his chair. It was a later night for them than usual to still be at the station but the amount of pressure that followed the news articles kept them at their desks. Dave looked at the clock and decided to call it a night. They could run in more circles the next day.

As he began packing up his things, he paused to listen to the radio chatter that was muffled through the static. He could only pick up bits and pieces, but something caught his ear. A woman was claiming that she had just been attacked in her home. Dave shot up out of his chair and ran over to Carol, who had placed the call. With a panicked look, he yelled out to her, "What was that call about?"

"A woman just rang in about an intruder in her house. She said he had a knife. I have teams responding now."

Sean came over to see what Dave was all about and overheard the conversation. He quickly responded to Carol, "What was the address?"

Carol read it off to the detectives and they ran out the door. If the situation was what they assumed, they were about to have their first real witness.

~ ~ ~

Tracy Vanderbelt was washing the dishes when she remembered it was Wednesday, trash night. She had just finished a pork dinner; one she had planned on making with her husband before he was called away on a work trip for the week. She finished washing her last pan and placed it on the drying rack. She took out a large piece of aluminum foil and covered the rest of the pork. She would have leftovers until the weekend. After finding an open spot for it in her refrigerator, she went back to the sink and washed her hands.

It was later than usual for her to have just finished eating dinner. With her husband gone, time seemed to go faster and tended to get away from her. She was reminded of the hour by the setting sun. The June sky was a picturesque pink and slowly growing darker. Tracy looked down at her overflowing trash can. It was usually her husband's task to take it out on Wednesdays. He often let procrastination win over his evening until he was forced to take it out before bed. Tonight, he wouldn't even have to worry about it.

Following in his example, rather than get it over with, she decided to make tea and relax in front of the T.V. for a while. Tracy walked over to her side kitchen cabinet for a cup when an unmistakable noise caught her attention. It was the sharp ring of breaking glass.

She stood perplexed in her kitchen while her mind searched for an explanation. Maybe a bird hit a window in another room or a glass she had left on an edge finally fell. She pondered over everything from night owls and nonexistent seismic faults to suicidal glassware before the worst idea crept into her mind. The thought that she was no longer alone in her home.

The realization came over her coldly. Her pulse quickened at the thought of it and she began to worry.

Tracy looked around her house with a sudden change in perspective. Her back door now felt like a good escape instead of a way to cool down the kitchen. The basement seemed like a trap with only one way out, and the front door, for the first time in her life, appeared to be holding her in instead of keeping others out.

The questioning side to her wouldn't have believed that there was something to be afraid of if she hadn't been reading the paper for the last four months. The story of the Garage Guerrilla was a constant conversation piece in the neighborhood and all over the community. She thought to herself how common it must be for women throughout Riverwood to hear a strange noise and grab the family gun or their best paring knife before investigating.

Now, she too, was holding a knife. She thought about grabbing the phone, but what would she say to the police? "I've heard a noise?" The embarrassment that would follow from causing a fuss over nothing kept her from reaching for it.

Yet, all that aside, she knew what she heard. She decided that she needed to stop being so skittish and go see it for herself. She had to come to her senses and take care of the problem as someone her age would be expected to do. She squeezed her knife tighter and called out softly around the corner into the front room.

"Hello?"

She listened intently for a scuffle, a breath, anything. She quickly reached her hand around and flipped the light switch. The room illuminated and she jumped back into the kitchen with her knife in front of her. She called out to the room again.

"Hello?"

She listened once more. Nothing. She decided she had to look in the room. She crept to the entryway of the kitchen and popped her head around the corner. She stared into an empty room. Seeing it so still gave her the chills when she was so certain it wouldn't be.

Tracy looked past the front door and shifted her focus to the one on the opposite side of the room, the door to the garage. A pit grew heavy in her stomach. What waited behind that door? Was it him?

She moved to the front door and checked if it was locked. It was. Her mind raced to the back door. Was it locked? It was. She was sure of it; she had locked it before dinner. She looked back to the garage door and her stomach knotted tighter. She remembered that she hadn't locked that door when she got home. If this man was on the other side of it, he could twist the handle and walk right in.

Tracy stared at the door, expecting it to make the next move. She slowly moved her way towards it, listening carefully after every step. She made it to the door and placed her ear to it, but her heart was pounding too loud for her to hear. She pulled her head away and tried to relax. She took a deep breath and placed her head back on the door, listening between her own breath for someone else's. A minute past and doubt began to come over her. Was she being foolish? Had there even been a sound? There had to have been. She was sure of it.

She put her head back to the door and listened past her beating heart through the thin wood and into the room. Nothing. The room was silent.

Slowly, Tracy reached down and twisted the lock on the door. Her nervous fingers worked awkwardly. She pulled her head away, placed her palm on the door and stared at it. She focused on the grooves in the wood, hoping she could feel past them for a presence on the other side. She again tried to calm herself down and put her head back on the door. Once more she heard nothing. Doubt came over her again. She began to wrestle with her own paranoia and argued with herself.

What if he's in there?

Even if he is, the door is locked. I can go back to the couch and relax.

No, I'll still have to take the trash out. Shit.

Tracy thought again about asking the operator for the police but shook it off. The police weren't in the business of checking out noises. She decided she was being foolish. She had to look, only for a second, just to see into the garage. Then, she could put herself at ease and get on with her evening.

She took a deep breath and put her hand on the door handle. She slid her hand over the lock. She would do it in one quick move; swing the door open, let the light from the front room spill into the garage just long enough to see, then slam the door. All she needed was a couple of seconds.

Her heart raced as her fingers grasped the lock and switched it over. She tightly grabbed the handle and quickly jerked the door open.

For Tracy, it felt like a slow-motion film. Each second slid by as if frame by frame. The door swung open. Tracy let it hit the backstop and froze. Adrenaline overwhelmed her. She stood face-to-face with a man. His eyes came to life, showing his intentions, and he lunged at her. His gloved right hand shot out for her throat and his left cocked back with a knife.

Instinctively, Tracy screamed and brought her knife down. The blade caught his hand and wedged an opening between his thumb and his index finger. His face twisted in pain and he reeled back to avoid another blow. Blood began to quickly pour out of his glove. Tracy saw her chance and slammed the door in his face. She threw her body weight into the door and locked it.

Her breathing was hysterical. Panic-stricken, she fought to catch her breath and looked for him through the windows. She worried about how else he would try to get into the house.

With her full weight against the door, Tracy waited for him to return. Tears were coming down her face and she knew she had to act if she wanted help. She sprang from the door over to the kitchen where she grabbed the phone and dialed the operator. As soon as the call connected, she frantically screamed, "Get me the police!"

~ ~ ~

Sean and Dave pulled up behind two patrol cars. They ran to the front door and pounded on it. An officer opened the door. They hurried inside and found a woman crying at her kitchen table next to a knife. She was wiping her tears as an officer tried to comfort her. Two other officers were investigating the house. Dave walked up to the table and asked the woman, "Ma'am, are you OK?"

She nodded, still shaking from the adrenaline. He looked around the kitchen and asked, "Where did you see him, Ma'am?"

She pointed out to the front room and replied, "The garage."

Sean and Dave walked back into her front room and saw blood droplets on the floor in front of the garage door. Sean walked over to the door and opened it. As he had expected, the garage was now empty. He looked over and found the light switch on the wall. He struck the switch, but the garage remained dark. He looked back at

Dave behind him, they both knew what that meant. He pulled out a flashlight and pointed it up to where the light would be and saw an empty socket. He moved his light across the floor and found a trail of blood leading to the side door. Its windowpane had been broken in. Sean looked back at Dave, confirming, "It was him."

The detectives knew time was against them. Their man was injured and on the run. They needed to get patrols out as quickly as possible. They turned back into the house. Sean called out to the officer, who let them in and said, "This was the Garage Killer. Get it out on the radio that we need as many guys on the streets as possible. Our man is injured and probably bleeding."

The officer ran out of the house and Sean and Dave walked back into the kitchen. Sean took a seat at the table next to the crying woman. She had just experienced the worst night of her life. As far as the detectives knew, she was the only survivor of their Garage Killer. Sean couldn't help but feel a little excited. This was the break that he and Dave needed, and he wanted to hear every detail the woman could give them. He pulled out a notepad and asked, "What's your name, Ma'am?"

She choked back a response, "Tracy Vanderbelt."

"Tracy, I know you're going through a lot right now, but we need you to tell us everything that just happened."

She closed her eyes and nodded. Sean began, "Were you able to see his face?"

Tracy nodded again.

"Could you describe him for me?"

"He had black hair and white skin."

"Any distinguishing features or facial hair?"

Tracy looked down and shook her head.

"Would you say he was White, Asian or Hispanic?"

Tracy seemed to have trouble remembering and then settled on. "White or Hispanic. I couldn't really tell."

"OK. What about eye color? Did you see his eyes?"

"They were dark. Almost black."

Sean jotted that down and continued. "Could you tell me about his build? Was he stocky, skinny, chubby?"

"He wasn't fat, but he wasn't really big. He was just intimidating."

Sean wrote *stocky*. "How old would you have guessed him to be?

"I don't know. He could have been in his twenties or thirties."

She was giving them a very vague description. Sean tried desperately to get something unique. He asked, "What were his clothes like? Can you describe them?"

"They were normal. Jeans and a T-shirt with an un-buttoned shirt on top but he was wearing gloves."

The detectives had assumed he had been wearing gloves. It explained their lack of prints. He wrote the clothing down and looked back at her to ask, "You struck him with that knife, didn't you?" Sean was pointing at the knife while he looked for cuts on Tracy.

She nodded.

"How did you know to grab the knife?"

"I heard glass breaking and thought that someone was getting into the house."

Finally, for once, the killer hadn't caught his victim by surprise. Sean asked, "Where did you get him with the knife?"

Tracy held her hand up as if the motion would help her remember. "I swung to my left side. So, it would've been his right hand."

"And where did you cut him on the right hand?"

Tracy closed her eyes. "He was reaching out for me and I brought the knife down on him. It got him between his thumb and his finger."

Sean pointed at the area she described on his own hand and said, "On top of the hand, right here?"

Tracy nodded, "Yes, right there."

Sean wrote the injury down in his notes before asking, "What did he do after you struck him?"

"His hand went limp and he turned away. That was when I closed the door on him and locked it."

It sounded like a quick series of events. Sean was confident he had heard what he needed. Finally, he asked, "Is that when you called the police?"

Tracy nodded once more.

It wasn't much of a description, but it built onto what the detectives had. Sean and Dave knew they needed to get the information out on the radio as quickly as possible. He closed his notebook, got up from the table and said, "Thank you, Tracy. Do you have anywhere you can go?"

She attempted to smile, signaling a yes. Sean looked over at the officer in the room and said, "Make sure the blood on the floor doesn't get cleaned up until the forensics guys get here. We need it for an ABO sample." The officer muttered, "Ok," and the detectives left him in the room with Tracy.

Out on the street, Sean and Dave could see Tracy's neighbors watching the house from their porches. They made it down to Dave's car and Sean grabbed for the radio. He needed to get the loose description of the attacker out to the patrols. Dave watched him as he did it. When he was finished Dave spoke his mind. "I think we have enough to go talk to Welch now."

Sean put the radio down and asked, "The cut?"

"He's either got it or he doesn't. With as much blood as we saw in there, it had to be a pretty good whack. Something like that would be hard to cover up."

Sean agreed. There was no way anyone could hide a wound like that. He responded, "That's a good idea, and if Christopher can get us a blood type from the pool of it in the garage, we'll actually have our first piece of evidence directly from the killer."

Once they had the killer's blood type, they could use it to narrow down their suspect search. It would save them days of work with their veteran angle or it could help implicate Welch.

As the detectives talked over their next steps, the forensics team and another police vehicle pulled up in front of the house. Lieutenant Harrison got out of the patrol car and started walking towards them. He looked alert and serious as he called out to them, "We heard you on the radio. What's the story?"

"Our guy was here," Dave replied. "He was waiting for the lady in the garage, like usual." She heard him break the glass on her garage door and met him at the door into the house with a knife."

The lieutenant's eyes widened. "And she's fine?"

"She's doing ok. He didn't touch her."

"We got every cruiser we can scanning the streets, and the K9 units are hitting the parks. Hopefully, that profile you gave will give us something. Do you think she can help make a composite?"

Sean sighed, "No. She couldn't remember his face. She was too shaken up."

Even though they only had a vague description, the

group felt hopeful. They knew the killer couldn't be far, but time was against them.

Harrison continued, "Chief Perry informed me that he got a call from the mayor. We've been approved to use a helicopter."

Sean and Dave weren't expecting to hear that. With the added help, they felt confident this was their chance to end the hunt once and for all. The lieutenant pointed down the street and said, "We'll have the chopper sweep the neighborhood and then hit every nook and cranny on its way east to Denver."

"Where do you want us?" replied Sean.

"Either checking the streets in your car or with the search parties in the parks; I'll leave it up to you."

"We'll probably hit the closest ditch trail and work our way into the parks. The patrols will have the streets covered."

Harrison nodded and looked at the detectives earnestly. "Good luck tonight. We all know we need it. Stay on the radios."

Sean and Dave parked their car around the corner from Tracy Vanderbelt's house at the entrance to the ditch trail. The street crossed over a small bridge that spanned the ditch and connected the neighborhood east to west. It made sense that their man was using the trails to get around unseen at night, but Dave still didn't know the real reason Sean was so adamant in exploring them.

They got out of their car and looked down the dark path, unsure which way to go. One end led them south, deeper into Riverwood, while the other end led them north. They decided to move south, further into the city. Dave grabbed a handheld radio and set the volume low. the detectives pulled out flashlights and clicked them on. The green opening came into view. Sean checked if his pistol was loaded and holstered it before starting down the path.

The trail was completely dark. In some spots, the large cottonwoods standing at the banks of the ditch formed a full canopy. The detectives could only see what their flashlights showed them. A cool breeze blew through the trees and ruffled the leaves around them as they moved deeper into the path, making it hard for them to listen for movement. They were alert and tried to push back the thought that the killer was watching them from somewhere hidden on the dark path. When the wind stopped blowing and the leaves quieted, it revealed the softer sound of the small stream below them. It was an ideal area to move unheard.

Twigs cracked nearby and their flashlights reflected against small orange eyes in the bushes. Raccoons and cats sporadically came into view before hiding back into the brush. Sean and Dave made it to a clearing in the trees as Dave's radio began to chatter. They could hear the beat of a distant helicopter. The search was on.

The detectives followed the ditch until it came into a much larger clearing. They had made it to the park. They could hear barking dogs and could see other flashlights searching the trees at the far end. One of the K9 teams. Sean and Dave worked their way towards them and waved their lights in the air — they didn't want to be mauled by one of their own dogs. The other men with lights called the dogs back and came to meet them.

The K9 group recognized the detectives. The point man called out to them. "Which way did you come from?"

Sean yelled back, "North, from the house."

The sound of the helicopter was growing louder. Now, they could see it in the distance over the treetops. The point man responded, "We're sweeping south. You're welcome to join."

Sean and Dave walked into the group. They could see restrained shepherds anxiously pulling towards them. They walked to the back of the K9 team and followed along. The sound from the helicopter became deafening and a searchlight lit up the park's open field before scanning the tree line. The dogs barked with excitement. No one in Riverwood would sleep tonight. It was two hours before midnight but the lights from almost every house were turning on. The team led the dogs to the south end of the park where they pulled them into another ditch trail that took them further into the city. Dave's radio chatter had become nonstop. He lowered the volume as much as he could so he could still focus on scanning the park.

As the group moved further south and the night pressed on, the detectives started to worry. Enough time had gone by and no one had spotted their man. The radio sounded off with directions and orders but no sightings. This was the closest they had ever been behind the killer, but it still wasn't enough. He somehow had the time to hide or escape, and the search teams were losing hope.

After a while, the K9 unit doubled back for Tracy's house. They searched the park once again and found nothing. Even with all the help, the killer had gotten away.

The next morning Sean and Dave were recuperating at their desks and sipping coffee. Although they came up empty-handed the night before, the attempt on Tracy Vanderbelt's life had revived the case. Their killer had acted sooner than normal, and it scared the detectives. In the past, he had waited weeks, or months, between his attacks, but the chance he had just taken was only a week after the death of Helen Philips. The detectives wondered if he was gaining confidence or caving easier into his urges.

Either way, knowing he had failed at an attempt was satisfying. His confidence had to be wounded, and for the first time, the killer had left behind physical evidence. The detectives felt they were finally starting to gain on him.

In their paperwork approach, Vincinni was taking the lead in reviewing the veteran criminal records. He and Hull had been painstakingly attacking the files, but it would be a slow go. They needed more time to build a comprehensive list. In the meantime, the days were dragging on and women were still being attacked.

Dave took a long gulp of strong coffee and looked over at Sean. "When do you want to go check out Welch?"

Sean tiredly rubbed his eyes. "They open at nine. We can call in then, see if he's working."

"Why wait? Why don't we go now and get him before work?"

Sean agreed with Dave. The sooner they knew about Welch the better. He replied, "Let's go check him out."

The detectives pulled up in front of the address Jack Barlow had given them. They looked onto a battered yard that led to a disheveled track house with fading blue paint. The home appeared to have never been re-painted, remodeled or kept up at all since it was sold in the 40s. The yard had a life of its own and was doing what it could to reclaim the basement windowsills.

Dave laid out his plan. "I'm going to go at this easy,

act like we're just asking folks if they saw anything strange last night. There isn't a soul in this city that didn't wake up to that helicopter."

It sounded like a good idea. They didn't know too much about Welch and they weren't sure how aggressive he could be. For self-assurance, Sean checked if his pistol was fully loaded and holstered it.

Dave got out of the car and headed for the door. He knocked twice, and the smell of bacon and cigarettes hit them as the door opened. A black-haired, clean-shaven and stocky man was on the other side of it. Welch looked unsure of the two detectives and asked, "Is there something I can do for you?"

Welch was speaking through a screen door. He leaned against his doorframe, blocking his right hand from the detectives' view. Dave started the conversation, "Good morning, sir. We're with the Riverwood Police. We're just checking on the neighborhood, seeing if anyone saw anything suspicious last night. A man hopping fences or being where he shouldn't?"

Welch looked surprised. "Is this about that helicopter last night?"

"Yes, sir, I think we kept the whole city up."

"Were you guys looking for that Garage Guerrilla from the paper?"

Dave nodded as he searched the man's face for a break in composure. Welch smiled and then shook his head. He replied, "No, I didn't see anything last night. Just couldn't sleep."

Sean didn't know what else Dave planned to ask Welch. They needed to see his right hand, otherwise, their visit was pointless. He spoke up from behind Dave, "Hey, I think I know you."

Welch squinted at him and Sean continued, "Yeah, you work at the mechanic shop, right? Fenders?"

Welch nodded.

"My wife brought her junker into you guys. Damn thing sounded like a junior high band. It's clean as a whistle now."

Dave listened to Sean and caught on to what he was doing. Welch smiled at the compliment and Sean went on, "I forgot to thank you guys myself. The damn job keeps me busy but man, I should shake your hand. You guys really did me a favor."

Sean reached out an inviting right hand towards the screen door and asked, "I don't think I caught your name. What was it?"

Welch looked at the hand through the screen and then cracked another smile. He replied, "It's Daryl." He pushed the screen open and put a clean right hand into Sean's.

Sean stared at the hand and never made eye contact throughout the handshake. His heart sank as he saw the healthy hand. Welch wasn't their man. He had been a waste of time. Sean thanked him again and the defeated detectives walked back to their car.

The lingering morale boost the detectives felt from the night before was fading. They were back to a case without a name to hold on to. Sean and Dave were eagerly anticipating the news from Christopher about the blood left at the crime scene, but when they stepped inside the station, they realized it would have to wait.

The switchboard was flooded with calls over the commotion from the night before. The added drama the helicopter search had caused was catching up with them and the detectives were forced to spend the rest of the day manning the phones. It turned into another day of sifting through complaints and conspiracies. Sean and Dave didn't get a break until the day was practically over.

When the calls finally died down, the detectives left to grab a bite to eat at the Ralston Cafe next door. The phones had taken the life out of them; once their food arrived, Sean and Dave barely touched their pancakes. Josie came by to fill up their coffees. Dave was oddly quiet, and she could tell the two seemed bothered.

"Long day?"

Dave didn't take his eyes off his plate. Sean looked over to her and reached out his coffee cup for a refill.

"Yeah," he replied, "a bit rough."

"I heard the helicopter last night and I saw the story in the afternoon paper."

Dave looked up from his plate to ask, "What'd the paper say?"

"It mentioned the helicopter and the murder last night."

Dave shook his head and looked back at his plate. "There wasn't a murder last night."

"The paper said there was."

"Well, the paper got it wrong. What paper was it?"

"*Rocky Mountain News*."

Dave smiled and looked at Sean. "Ed being Ed. That guy loves writing up a story."

Josie took her coffee pot and walked away to another table. Dave watched her walk away and went back to staring at his food. He could feel a growing frustration boiling out of him. He hotly looked up at Sean and said, "Can you believe Ed? How can that guy even call himself a journalist?"

Sean shook his head and didn't respond. Dave's anger built even more until it got him out of his seat and up to go grab the paper. He found the newsstand in the front of the restaurant and grabbed Thursday's afternoon issue of the *Rocky Mountain News*.

The title made his stomach drop. It read, "Amber Ridge Woman Butchered." He quickly scanned the words below it and ran it over to the table. Dave threw the paper down and said, "Sean, look at this."

Sean's eyes went wide as he saw the headline. Amber Ridge was the smaller city just north of Riverwood. As the two cities expanded, their housing developments reached into each other and blended together. He stared back at Dave. "What's it say?"

"It mentions our night search and calls our use of the helicopter irresponsible."

Sean didn't care about Ed's opinion; he wanted to hear about the murder. He asked again, "What does it say about the woman?"

"It says a woman was murdered in front of her home last night."

Dave handed the paper over across the table. Sean grabbed it and quickly read through the article. It detailed the brutal stabbing of a mother outside of her home in the late hours of Wednesday night.

"It wasn't in a garage," said Sean as he read the article.

He continued reading but abruptly stopped when one sentence caught his eye.

Is this the work of the Riverwood Garage Guerrilla? Amber Ridge Investigators are leaving all options on the table.

Sean looked up at Dave and said, "Ed's already calling this our guy. We didn't even get a call."

"Why would we have? It was in Amber Ridge."

Sean put his eyes back on the article. He needed to

know everything he could about the murder. As Dave watched him read, a question came to his mind that bothered him. He asked, "How did he get the woman out of the house?"

Sean read on until he found the answer and then looked up at Dave. "Apparently five houses on that street had their hoses turned on. The poor woman went outside to turn the hose off."

Dave had a curious look on his face. He closed his eyes and rubbed them. The murder seemed random and disorganized. If five houses were hit, then there wasn't a specific target. How could Ed have called it the garage killer? Their man always had a plan and a target, and he never committed a crime in the open. This murder was the opposite, out in a front yard, unplanned and without a specific target.

Dave shook his head. "What makes Ed think this murder was done by our Garage Killer?"

Sean thought about the question and took a sip of his freshly poured coffee. He replied, "We should have gone north."

"What?"

Sean explained, "Last night. We could have gone north or south. We went south and met up with the K9 unit. What would have happened if we went north?"

Dave's curiosity turned to concern. He asked, "You think he took the ditch trail north into Amber Ridge?"

"Of course he did. We searched all of Riverwood. We even had a bird in the sky, and we came up with nothing." Sean sat back and folded his arms. "I think that's because we didn't have anyone to find in Riverwood. We assumed he was going back towards Denver, while in reality, he went a few miles north and slipped into Amber Ridge. He knew that we wouldn't be looking in a different jurisdiction."

"That still doesn't explain the hose or the murder in the front yard."

"I think it does. Think about it. He was confident in his method. He planned his fourth murder and went to see it out, but it failed. The lady heard him coming and met him at the door with the knife, so he ran. He was mad and desperate, and he had to fix his broken ego. So, he escaped to where he knew we wouldn't be looking for him and he came up with a new plan."

Dave stared at Sean and thought about it. As much as he didn't like what Sean was saying, it made sense. The crime was random enough to make it look desperate. Dave replied, "It's possible, but Ed doesn't know all of that. He only knows about the murder and the helicopter. How'd he pick our guy?"

Sean smiled at him. "The Garage Killer, or Ed's 'Garage Guerrilla', is the only boogie man in town. He's got no other names to drop."

Dave shook his head and took a sip of coffee. The

extra caffeine jumbled something loose and he started to think ahead. He stated to Sean, "The county forensics team would've responded to that murder."

Sean nodded as he got on the same page. If their man committed this murder, they needed more information to confirm it. And they knew where to find it, Mark and Christopher.

Chapter 10

J ake was listening intently. His eyes were glued to the desk phone in front of him. Sean Kennedy was alive, and they were talking to him.

Spears cleared his throat and explained the call, "Mr. Kennedy, We've been reviewing cold cases here at the station and a couple of your older cases have caught our eye. The so-called, 'Garage Guerrilla' murders."

The old man listened on the other line. He was clearly surprised by the call, but he was curious as to what they wanted from him. He replied, "Yeah, those were mine. What can I do for you captain?"

"Well, sir, we are going to run the evidence left in storage from those three murders through modern DNA testing, and we wanted to speak with you beforehand to see if you had any added insights we might not have access to in the paperwork."

Sean made a wheezing sound over the phone. It was hard to tell if it was a cough or laugh. He replied, "Did you say three?"

"Yes, sir, three cases."

"There were more than three cases."

Spears looked up at Jake. The young detective didn't know what to say. He had gone through the rest of the cold cases from 1969, but there had been only three garage murders. He returned a puzzled look. Spears leaned over the phone and said, "I'm sorry sir, did you say, 'more than three'?"

"Yes, by my count we had five."

Spears looked back over at Jake. Again, he returned a confused look, but this time he leaned forward to speak on the phone. "Sir, my name is Jake Caldwell. I'm the detective who pulled up these cases. Our records only show three homicides that took place in garages in 1969. Are we supposed to find more?"

"No detective, you found all of the garage murders. The killer was fairly adaptive. He changed his M.O. after he had a mishap."

Jake leaned away from the phone and turned the call back over to Spears. He hadn't expected to hear that. The captain felt they had listened to enough. He decided it would be better to meet with the old man. He asked, "Sir, it sounds like there's a lot we don't know. Is there any chance you have the time to meet?"

"Yeah, I can do that. As long as it's not too late in the afternoon."

"We can keep a morning open. What day works best for you?"

"To be honest, captain. I'm free right now. How's today work?"

Spears was surprised by the quick turnaround, but he welcomed the idea. He looked up at Jake as he responded, "Today works well. Do you want to meet us at the station?"

"I'd rather avoid the station. How about the diner next door?"

The diner was practically an extension to the station, it was all the same for Spears. "That works with us," He responded. "How soon should we walk over?"

"I'll see you in thirty minutes, captain."

Bacon, grease and red booths. The diner hadn't changed in fifty years. Sean Kennedy sat in his car in the parking lot, reminiscing about the old place. This was where he spent countless hours. For years, it had been his refuge where he went to unwind and forget about his troubles. He always found it hard to be stressed with a coffee in his hand, the smell of bacon in his nose and a plate of pancakes coming his way. He knew if he had to discuss the Garage Guerrilla, he'd rather do it in the comfort of the diner. It was better there than in the stuffiness of the station, and it only seemed fitting. He had done most of his thinking about the case at the diner to begin with, and he figured it would jog old memories.

Sean took a deep breath and stepped out of his car. He walked into the diner and saw two men sitting side by side in a booth at the back. After explaining he was there to meet a man named Spears, the doorman pointed him in their direction. Sean slowly made his way over and took a seat at the open end of the table. He gave the men a nod.

"Gentlemen. So, you're the ones looking into my old cases?"

Spears introduced Jake and himself. "I'm Captain Alonzo Spears, and this is one of our new detectives, Jake Caldwell."

A large woman approached the table. She took a look at Spears and Jake and shrugged them off once she saw the old man. She said, "Sean, how you doing, honey? Can I start you with a coffee?"

The old man smiled back. "Sure thing, Josie."

Jake tried not to stare at her flabby arms. The woman was enormous. She perfectly fit the stereotype of an old diner waitress. She spoke in a rough character that carried a forced side of sweetness. Josie took their orders and vanished into the kitchen.

Spears pulled out a pen and paper and started the

conversation. "Mr. Kennedy," He said, "thanks for meeting us. On the phone, you mentioned there were more than just three murders — an additional two?"

Josie came back and set down a tray of water and coffee. Sean grabbed a coffee and then responded, "That's right. We had five, but one of them didn't happen in Riverwood. It was up north in Amber Ridge."

Spears started taking notes and replied, "You mentioned that the offender had changed his M.O. What exactly did that entail?"

"As I'm sure you've noticed, for each garage murder, he did everything the same. He would watch his victim, learn their schedules and then break the glass on their garage side door to allow himself in. Every time, he removed the garage light and waited his victim out until they followed their schedule and came to him."

Sean took a sip of his coffee and continued, "But on his fourth attempt, it didn't go as planned for him. The woman heard him break the glass to her garage door. She met him at the house door with a knife and cut him. She called us and we turned the city inside out looking for him. However, that same night, in what we assumed was some sick form of vengeance, he slipped into Amber Ridge to find another victim."

Jake interjected, "And that's when he changed his M.O.?"

Sean nodded, "He abandoned his tested method and

instead turned on the hoses to five houses on the same street, in the hopes that a woman inside one of them would come out to turn hers off. And one did. When we first got the news, we were on the fence about whether or not it was him. It wasn't his style, but it was his type of victim and close to his area. It wasn't long after, that hoses began to turn on at night throughout Riverwood. That's when we knew it was him. It was as if he was sending us a message. It was about a month later when he claimed another victim in Riverwood. After that, everything went back to normal, and he vanished."

Spears finished writing and asked Sean, "So he changed his method in desperation?"

"The first time, yes. After that, he began to target single houses and appeared to follow a plan again."

Jake had a question bugging him. "Why didn't he go all the way into the houses? If he had been watching his victims, he would've known they were alone."

Sean sighed, "This man was a coward. Most of us assumed that he didn't have the confidence to go into the houses. He never took chances with confrontation. Even if he did know his victims' schedules, he could never know what was in the house without going inside, and that made it unpredictable for him. In the garage, he had the elements of fear and surprise. The garage was his controlled space. He had a clear way out and he always knew what was coming."

Spears added onto Jake's question, "But then, with the garden hoses, he abandons his controlled space?"

"After he was attacked in a garage his controlled space became unpredictable. Everyone in the city knew about him and what he was doing. He never went back to the garage. He lost confidence in it. So, he tried to find a safer way to get to his victims without having to break into their homes. That method was with the garden hose, but it too was unpredictable, and I think that's why he stopped."

Josie came back to the table and dropped off three hot plates of food. Jake was hungry but too interested to eat. He couldn't get over the idea of the killer getting away unseen from his reconnaissance. He asked Sean, "If the killer was watching his victims to the point where he knew their nightly schedules, how was he not reported as a suspicious person?"

Sean took a bite of potatoes and swallowed, before saying, "At some point in time he might have been, but it was a different era. It wasn't uncommon to hear about peeping toms or a nosey neighbor. All of that didn't have the stigma it does today."

"Even after two murders?"

Sean put down his fork so he could focus on his answer. He replied, "At that point, no. We weren't sure how he was getting away with it. After the second murder, the newspapers had done a good job of scaring the public. We were often so swamped with calls we couldn't leave our desks. Paranoia was rampant. How he chose his victims, or even why, we never truly understood."

Spears played with his food while he thought about what Sean was telling them. He asked, "You said that on his fourth attempt the woman cut him. Did you get any of the blood?"

"We did. I'm sure the sample doesn't exist anymore, but I can tell you his blood type was A positive."

Spears wrote it down and replied, "Where did she cut him?"

Sean laughed. The question brought back embarrassing memories. He replied, "She got him on the right hand. Right in between his thumb and index finger. I've been staring at handshakes ever since."

Spears was amused by the comment. "Have you ever seen a scar like that?"

"Sure. A couple of times, as a matter of fact," sighed Sean, "the most embarrassing one was on a cruise in '98. Turned out the guy had a shop class accident back in high school, but I had already made things good and awkward before I found that out."

The table laughed. Jake thought of a question and asked, "So, he was bleeding the night he committed the murder in Amber Ridge?"

Sean nodded, "He had bled pretty good at the house."

"So, there's a chance he bled on his victim?"

"There's a chance, but back then the forensic pathologist didn't find anything."

Spears found that interesting, but he wanted to know more about what Sean thought of the killer. Spears asked, "You said he didn't have the confidence to continue. Is that really what you think made him stop? Most of these guys can't stop. Is it possible that he just went somewhere else?"

Sean thought about the question but shook his head and replied, "I guess there's a chance that he went somewhere else, but we were never aware of that. Here, things got too hot for him. The public was in a frenzy. People were staying up all night, watching their streets. Guys would get called in on just from staying in their cars to finish a cigarette. We had a helicopter that would go out three times a week, with a spotlight and the whole works. The killer couldn't play his games anymore. As much of a coward as he was, he had to hang it up."

Jake was itching to get his hands on that Amber Ridge case. Even though Sean had said the coroner never found A positive blood, he still had hope, but first, he needed to test Riverwood cases. They worked on their food and continued to chat with the old man in between bites. After a while, they began to slow down.

Sean sat back in his booth and smiled at Spears and Jake. He said, "I hope you two get what you're looking for. God knows it got the best of me." The old man nostalgically looked about the place and then smiled off his memories and said, "When I retired, I thought the case retired with me. I didn't think anyone would ever look into it again. I took all my boxes of witness files, suspect follow-ups and everything else when I left. My whole basement is Garage Guerrilla. I thought I took what mattered to the case, but if you two are right, then all I needed was a bloody T-shirt."

Jake wondered how many hours, *days*, of Sean's life the old man had devoted to the case Jake had only just stumbled upon. He imagined lazy Sundays for the old man where memories suddenly felt significant or sleepless nights when the case wouldn't let him have his peace. He looked back at Sean admiringly and replied, "Well, sir, if it works out the way we hope it does, you'll be the first one we call."

Back at the station, Jake hurried to the case room and started flipping through the files from 1969. He needed to find the murder that Sean Kennedy had just told them was part of the Garage Guerrilla case. Briefly remembering the files he had previously read, Jake ran his fingers over them and pulled out a case titled, "Janet Oliver Homicide July 9, 1969." Spears was standing over his shoulder. They opened the file and Jake skimmed the summary. He said, "This is it. This is the second hose murder he was talking about."

Spears squinted at the paper but couldn't read anything. Jake flipped the file to the evidence log and looked
it over while the captain waited impatiently behind him.

"Well? Do they have anything?"

"They have her clothing in the warehouse."

Jake gave the file to Spears to see for himself. Spears
grabbed the file and quickly flipped through it. He turned
it over and read the evidence log. Satisfied, he closed the
file and looked back at Jake.

"Ok. This is it. Now comes the fun part. Now we go
to the warehouse."

Jake was beyond excited. He couldn't believe they
were actually going to go through with it. It was the
moment he had been waiting for. He closed the 1969 case
cabinet and followed Spears out of the room.

Chapter 11

Sean and Dave headed to the crime lab after they left the Ralston Cafe. They hoped they could get a word in with Christopher about the Amber Ridge homicide before he called it a night. The crime lab always worked a long shift the day after a murder.

The detectives ascended the stairs and made it to Christopher's desk. The poor man was hunched over a stack of papers. He looked up and, at first, seemed surprised to see Sean and Dave, but then smiled and said, "I thought you two would be coming around."

The detectives sat in the chairs in front of him and Dave replied, "Sounds like you had your hands full last night."

"I could've said the same to you. I tell you, this place is just getting crazier and crazier!"

"Well, what'd it look like? Is there any chance it's our guy?"

Christopher sighed heavily, "It feels logical to assume so, but unfortunately we don't have anything to back it up physically." He paused and let his statement settle in before continuing. "We don't have a murder weapon, fingerprints or footprints. Once again we have nothing."

Sean replied, "What about the blood your guys got from the house we were at?"

"That, we do have. We ran it this morning."

Sean and Dave were both on the edge of their seats. Christopher looked down at his notes and read off, "A positive."

Sean said it back to him to confirm, "A positive?"

Christopher nodded.

Dave took out his notebook and wrote the blood type down, then asked, "Have you spoken to Mark? Was he able to find A positive blood on the victim?"

"I don't know yet. He wasn't done when I talked to him."

Dave looked over at Sean and said, "We need to get over there."

Sean agreed. If their killer really was responsible for the newest murder, gaining a physical link would be paramount. The detectives got out of their chairs and thanked Christopher. As usual, Sean yelled back to him as they left, "We'll let you know what we find out."

Sean and Dave walked out of the crime lab and made

it over to the coroner's office. They had high hopes for Mark. They had both seen how bad the killer had bled at Tracy Vanderbelt's house and if that same man later committed a violent murder, his blood would have gotten all over his victim.

They walked down a familiar corridor and opened the double doors. Mark stared at them and said, "I wasn't expecting you two."

The detectives didn't reply. They assumed that the circumstances did the talking for them. Mark quickly got the idea and walked over to the body drawer holding the latest victim. He opened it up and a mangled corpse came into view. Mark began, "This is Anna Schneider. She was stabbed twelve times and her throat was cut. She showed signs of a struggle and, much like your other victims, the weapon was a kitchen knife. Time of death was 9 p.m. to 10 p.m. and we determined her blood type was O positive."

"O positive is all you found?" asked Dave.

"Yes. O positive was all that we found."

Even after Mark's answer, Dave pointlessly went on. "We have reason to believe that the man who killed this woman was bleeding profusely. There were no other traces of another blood type?"

Mark returned a sullen look and replied, "Her clothing was soaked in her own blood."

Sean put his head in his hands. Every time he felt

like they were getting somewhere with the case they found themselves nowhere. Time was against them and they needed to dig up something they could use. Vincinni claimed they still had weeks of work ahead of them in order to get through all the veteran criminal records, but it was quickly becoming their only option. It was a painstaking process, but they were desperate. They were willing to do anything to get a couple of names on a list. The detectives thanked Mark for his time and called it a night.

~ ~ ~

It was a month later, close to midnight, on Tuesday, July 8, 1969, when eleven-year-old Michael Martin couldn't sleep. Beyond his own imagination, he had real things to be afraid of at night. Every kid in Riverwood talked about the Garage Guerrilla. It was summertime but schoolyard stories were still amplified, boasted and shared. In their eyes he wasn't after women, he was really after them.

The appearance of the police search helicopter three times a week didn't help, either. It always came at random, unannounced to the public, and flew low with two scanning searchlights poised to radio in a pursuit for the nearby patrols. Its loud guttural sound beat against window pains and shook houses. Those were sleepless nights. Even in the distance, it resonated at a high pitch that became unmistakable as a warning for the coming disturbance. Dogs whimpered and barked, babies cried, and eyes ran bloodshot.

The far-off cry of the engine kept Mikey up. The sound took his imagination to the ditch trail, every kid's escape from watchful eyes behind the cover of the cottonwood trees. The spot where they swung on their tire swing late at night when they were too tired to jump the fence to the drive-in.

No one dared to go there now. This summer, the once-wooded refuge was only used as a quick adrenaline-filled shortcut to another part of the neighborhood. The tire swing sat empty.

Mikey swore he wouldn't go back through it at night after the last time he used it to get home from baseball. The path was dark and a bit more humid than the rest of the neighborhood. Its only light source was the moon. No streetlights made it through the cottonwoods. He remembered pausing on the sidewalk and looking down the leafy trail before sprinting down it. His footsteps echoed in front of him, silencing the crickets, leaving only the sound of the creek.

It was a calm, windless night but when he came to the familiar clearing with the tire swing, he stopped. Empty, it was in full pendulum, bobbing the branch it was tied to at every crest of its swing. The moon completely illuminated him in the clearing. It felt like a spotlight. A paranoia came over him that he was being watched; he couldn't think away the idea that this was a trap set specially for him. Mikey couldn't stand being there any longer and fear made him run. Against his better judgment, he sprinted ahead into the darkness. Eyes darting about as he ran, looking for movement, a shadow, anything.

That had been three weeks ago, just after school had gotten out, and he hadn't been back since, but now he was lying awake thinking about it. He wondered what walked the path now, hiding from the distant helicopter and police cruisers.

Mikey was trying to hold his breath and listen through his open window. His eyes stared out into the night just beyond his lightly colored drapes. The faint streetlight in front of their house fell on his window and let him see through the thin linen. His room faced the street. He was trying to pinpoint how far away the helicopter was from its echo when something else caught his ear. The sound of a footstep softly planting in the grass.

Mikey held his breath again and tried to focus while he stared at the window. Another footstep came closer. His mind wasn't playing tricks on him. Someone was there. He breathed slowly, waiting for the next one. It didn't immediately come. He began to relax until they quickly came back. Heavy and crackling footsteps, now on the lava rocks his dad placed around the house.

Mikey's heart began to race. He kept his eyes on the window and tried his best not to make a sound. The crackling was getting closer. A shadow slowly crept in front of the window. It was followed by a solid, dark silhouette. Mikey's heart practically stopped. He was lying still but felt paralyzed. The figured bent below the window and the screeching sound of the hose nozzle in his front yard turning over cut through the silence. Each twist of the handle sounded like nails on a chalkboard, raising the hairs on the back of his neck.

Mikey couldn't hold his breath anymore. He exhaled and was terrified that this man could hear him breathing. He couldn't hear beyond his own heartbeat, it had traveled through his chest and played in his ear. The sound of the nozzle turning over stopped and the figure appeared back in the window. It stood in silhouette looking through the thin drapes as if it could see him lying there.

He pretended to close his eyes, but Mikey could feel the man staring back at him. His presence occupied the room. He tried desperately not to move, not to breathe, not to think. Mikey's heart was beating so loud that he thought the man could hear it.

Suddenly, an abrupt light came through his window. It was the scanning light of the helicopter. Mikey heard the crackling of the lava rocks and the figure was gone.

The spotlight wandered past his room as the helicopter came closer. He still pretended to sleep, wishing the whole thing would be over. In his fear, he had blocked out the sound of the incoming helicopter. Its loud quick whips were coming closer, hard to ignore now.

The helicopter passed overhead, and the spotlight vanished. With the noise gone Mikey could hear the sound of the hose running. He closed his eyes tight and pulled the covers over his head.

Mikey woke up the next morning at 7 a.m. He crept past his dad, who was making a pot of coffee, and walked out the front door. His lawn had turned into a swamp. The grass in front of his bedroom was completely flooded and the hose was still spilling out. He trudged through the mess, turned the hose off and went back inside.

~ ~ ~

Dave walked around the corner from Carol's desk with a worried look on his face. Sean was slouched over paperwork and going over a few of the veterans Vincinni had rejected as persons of interest. Dave crashed into his seat dramatically and said, "That was another call about a hose being turned on," he sighed. "That's the fourth one this week."

The news caught Sean's attention. He lifted his head from his paperwork and replied, "We haven't had this happen in five weeks."

"The question is, are these kids playing tricks on neighbors and friends, or is this the real deal?"

Sean pointed at the files on his desk, "There were two months between Abigail Thompson and Kathrine Sandoval, right? And a month between Sandoval and Philips?"

"Yeah, that sounds right."

"His move into Amber Ridge, if that was really him was just about a month ago. The timing is right."

"The timing does seem to match a pattern, but why isn't he going back into garages? Why the hose?"

Sean leaned back in his chair and said, "Think about it. The community is still on high alert. He can't stake out houses and play his garage game like he could before."

"True, but he seems to be targeting houses again. The mornings we do get a call he's only hit one, not a whole block."

"He never broke into two garages in the same week. That makes me think these are still a bit random, even though he seems to be singling out a house."

Dave sighed, "Either way, I don't like it. We're lucky we aren't responding to those houses for a homicide already. I feel like it's only a matter of time. Can we get the chopper out full-time?"

The Riverwood PD had cycled the helicopter out at random throughout the weeks in an attempt to keep costs down. The mayor had decided the city couldn't afford to fly it every night. Sean shook his head and replied, "I don't think so. Lieutenant Harrison said he already spoke to Chief Perry about it. We only get the three nights."

"I guess we can have a patrol circle over there a couple of times."

They had been changing up patrol routes nightly in an effort to spread out their presence and keep the city at ease. But they both knew their patrols couldn't be everywhere. There would always be blind spots.

In the meantime, they continued to work on their paperwork angle. Vincinni had gone through most of the criminal records and, slowly but surely, they began to build a list. They found three main persons of interest from the process. Veterans who fit the bill, men with A positive blood whose records were peppered with burglary and sexual assault, even one charged with murder.

Vincinni had followed up on two of them already. One, a veteran with a dishonorable discharge from Korea — a 36-year-old homeless man whose life had crawled inside a bottle. He was living under a bridge over a nearby river. His conspicuousness ruled out his ability to go unnoticed watching houses in the street but beyond that, he had a scarless right hand. Vincinni left him where he found him.

The second was a younger man. A recent Vietnam veteran who turned to a life of crime after he got back from the war. He had a long record of breaking and entering and had found his way as a garbage man for a private dump. The fact that he was in a truck cruising the city had caught Vincinni's eye. He knew the streets and had the chance to look into the houses he serviced unnoticed. Being that the first murder occurred while the victim was taking out the trash, it made sense that a garbage man knew when to expect her. But when Vincinni finally met him, he was a letdown. The guy was pushing well over two hundred pounds and had a clean right hand. He couldn't have been the guy.

So, they were left with the third. A man who had a dishonorable discharge from Vietnam for murdering a prostitute in Saigon. He'd still be serving his sentence if it wasn't for a lawyer who found him an early way out. He was now back in Riverwood, still getting into trouble. His record was peppered with run-ins with the law. His most recent stint had been a break-and-enter, for which he was still on parole.

However, Sean didn't like him as a suspect. According to Sean, he had two major flaws. He had actually broken into a house and not just the garage, and he had been *caught*. The murderer they were after seemed too smart to make the mistakes this guy had, but Vincinni argued he had to have learned it somewhere.

The man was now a welder for a mom-and-pop contractor in the area. Being that he had a violent reputation, they couldn't expect him to be unarmed, so they figured it was smarter to talk to him in public. Vincinni had gotten the address to the construction site where the man was working so they could speak to him when the timing was right. With phone calls coming in about hoses in Riverwood, now felt like the best time.

Sean and Dave planned to go through his paperwork again and hoped to move him from a person of interest to a full-on suspect once they spoke to him the next morning. They were set to hit the job site before the sun rose and before his coffee had set in. They figured it was best to get him early. All they needed to do was to get through one more night.

~ ~ ~

It was later that evening, just after an episode of *The Beverly Hillbillies*, when Janet Oliver decided to put her kids to bed. It was getting late for her small five-year-old daughter and her eight-year-old son. Even though school was out for the summer she still liked to keep them on a normal routine to help make her days feel organized. She and her husband had to work in the morning, and she couldn't sleep when little feet were running around accompanied by sporadic giggles.

Janet's husband, Sam, had decided it was time for him to crawl into bed once the kids were asleep, but Janet wanted to stay up. It was Wednesday, after nine o'clock, which meant a new show she had taken a liking to would be on for the next hour. CBS's *Medical Center*. She didn't watch it every week but when she found the time and wanted to relax for a while, she enjoyed turning it on. It was her quiet celebration that she was halfway through the week.

She salvaged what was left of the wine they had at dinner and settled into a living room all of her own. A fast forty-five minutes later, she was still on the couch wishing she had another hour. It was getting close to 10 p.m. and well past her usual bedtime. She looked down at her empty wine glass, disappointed that the good times were over. Her bed was beginning to sound enticing. Her glass of wine wasn't helping her stay awake and her eyes felt heavy.

Janet walked over to the kitchen to clean out her glass. She scrubbed it out and stood for a second, admiring the cool breeze coming in from the open window. It had a faint smell of rain, brought on by a summer night thunderstorm. She walked back to the T.V. and turned it off. She looked about the room, making sure that she hadn't left anything behind before putting her hand out for the living room light switch. Janet hit the light and turned for the hall but paused at the sound of running water.

She must have left the faucet on when she cleaned her wine glass. She walked through the dark house and into the kitchen. There she found the sink how she'd left it, spotless and not running. The sound was more pronounced here. She looked around until she realized it had to be coming from outside the kitchen window. For a moment she couldn't imagine what the sound could be. Perhaps a busted pipe? She thought about waking Sam but quickly realized it was coming from the garden hose. She sometimes left the hose running after watering the garden. Janet decided to take care of it herself.

She walked to the front door and unlocked it. She heard the sound of the bark rustling underneath the hose. She assumed it had to be flooding the yard. She looked back out the open window but saw nothing. She knew the sooner she was back inside, the sooner she could get to bed. Janet slipped her shoes on and opened the door.

~   ~   ~

It was 10:46 p.m. when Sean received the call. He hung the phone up quietly, but he imagined throwing it against the wall. If it wasn't for his wife, Judy, he would've yelled loud enough to wake the whole neighborhood.

He didn't talk long on the phone but when he was told that the victim was found outside her home, stabbed and in a swamp from her running garden hose, he felt nothing but rage. His greatest fears had been realized. They had seen the warning signs but moving the patrols around hadn't been enough. He grabbed his things and sped off to 2025 Anza Street.

Christopher's guys got there at the same time as the detectives. The team had grown in size since the first murder, but the extra numbers didn't seem to be helping.

No one had any idea how to approach the mess they were in.

Hull and Vincinni stayed back and let Sean and Dave put a plan together. They walked over to meet with Christopher. A sharp screeching sound made them all look down the street at another police car burning rubber in their direction. The car dramatically stopped in front of the house. Lieutenant Harrison practically ripped the door off of the car as he got out of it. He ran over to the detectives wild-eyed and pointed at Hull and Vincinni. Harrison yelled, "What are you doing standing around?"

The detectives looked startled and confused. The lieutenant barked again, "We have a potential garage killer case that just happened thirty minutes ago and you two aren't out looking for him?"

The detectives stared back, unsure how to respond. They thought they were supposed to back up Sean and Dave. Harrison continued, "Kennedy and Maxwell got this. We need everyone we can out on the hunt right now. The chopper is fueling up and the dogs are hitting the parks, you two need to join the search. Go!"

Hull and Vincinni looked upset but hustled over to their car and got on the radio. Harrison walked over to Sean and Dave and gestured for Christopher to come over. He spoke calmly but directly. "I need this report to look clean. There'll be a lot of eyes on this. Christopher, you were at the murder in Amber Ridge a month ago so take the lead where you need to. I'm going to go out and join the K9 teams. We have officers consoling the family and we need to clean this up before we let the kids outside or gather a crowd. Make it sharp, make it quick. I'll be on the radio."

With that, the lieutenant hurried back down to his car and sped off. Christopher looked over at Sean and Dave and said, "Come on, let's get this over with."

The group pulled out their notepads, walked up the driveway and stepped onto the grass. Their shoes immediately sunk into the mud. They trudged up to the bark perimeter surrounding the home and came upon the body below the garden hose. Christopher turned on his flashlight and illuminated the poor woman. His team began to take photographs. He knelt down to look at her hands, but they were covered in mud.

Christopher scanned the area around the house with his flashlight. The garden hose was hidden by a large blue spruce that sat low and flat just beyond the laid bark. They all noticed how ideal a hiding place it was. Sean shook his head and said, "Without that flashlight, it would've been pitch black behind there."

They walked behind the tree, leaving Christopher's team with the body. Christopher moved his flashlight to a dirt area near the tree, catching distinct shoeprints pressed into the ground in the center of the light. He moved closer and pulled out a measuring tape, carefully kneeling beside the prints to record their size. He scribbled into his notebook and shook his head. "Would you look at that. They're size tens."

Sean stared at the shoe prints and looked over in the direction they were facing. It had a clear view of the living room. He could see the husband sitting on the couch with the officers inside. Sean sighed, "The guy was watching them." He looked back at Christopher and Dave. "No one has found a murder weapon but I'm betting it was a kitchen knife."

Christopher took a picture of the shoe prints with his tape on them and they moved back to the body. One of his investigators called out to them as they returned. "Look at the bark," he directed. "It's barely disturbed. Doesn't look like there was much of a struggle."

Christopher stopped and looked at the ground around the body. Sean noted the comment and the group headed towards the front door. As Christopher walked past his team, he said to them, "There are some shoe prints behind the tree over there. Go see if you can find anymore. Take a lot of pictures. Coroner's truck is coming soon and taking the body right away, so get what you need."

His guys nodded at him and left to find the prints. Stepping inside the house Christopher let Sean and Dave lead the way and said, "Dealing with people is more your guys' thing. I'll hang back and take notes."

Dave walked ahead and confronted the husband. The man was overcome with shock and was staring at his shoes. Dave reached out a handshake to try and snap him out of it. "Mr. Oliver, My name is Dave Maxwell. I'm sorry for your loss."

The man looked up expressionless and shook Dave's hand. The detectives took a seat on the other chairs in the living room while Christopher roamed the house. Sean spoke first. "Mr. Oliver, my name is Sean Kennedy. I know everything is a blur right now, but we need to put together your wife's evening."

The man didn't respond and dropped his head back down. Sean continued, "Mr. Oliver, you got in touch with our dispatch at just after 10:30 p.m. What was it that made you go outside? Did you hear the struggle?"

Sam Oliver slowly lifted his head and looked at Sean. His voice was distant and quiet. "No, I was in bed. Janet usually comes to bed around 9:30 p.m. Maybe a noise woke me up, but I don't remember hearing anything, I just remember looking over at the clock and deciding to go check on her."

Sean was taking notes as the man talked. He finished writing and asked, "Did you hear anything then? What made you go outside?"

The man's expression still hadn't changed. He calmly responded, "I couldn't find her in the house. I heard the hose running from the kitchen and that's when I found her."

Sean tried to think of the easiest way to ask his next question, but he knew no matter how he phrased it, it would be difficult. "Had she already passed?"

Mr. Oliver nodded.

"Did you see anyone outside?"

The man shook his head.

Sean scribbled in his notepad and looked back over at Mr. Oliver. "What were you doing before you went to bed?"

Oliver shrugged his shoulders. "We were watching television. *The Beverly Hillbillies.* We put the kids to bed, then I went to bed. Janet stayed up."

"What time was that?"

"Maybe around nine. Just after the show was done."

Dave was looking around the home and listening to the conversation. He decided to ask a question of his own. "Mr. Oliver, did you ever see anyone outside of your house? Maybe a kid or an admirer? A peeping Tom?"

The man looked over at Dave and said, "No. Nothing like that."

Sean butted in again, "Does your wife usually stay up later than you? Is she the one who locks the doors and turns out the lights?"

Oliver looked back down at his shoes. "Sometimes."

They could tell it was going to be hard to get anything of use out of the man. Despite their hopes, the husband hadn't witnessed anything unusual and his grief was coming on hard. Dave tried to comfort him before they moved on. "Mr. Oliver, we're going to do everything we can to find your wife's murderer. We're going to be working around the clock on this."

Sam Oliver continued to stare at his shoes and didn't respond. Dave gave Sean a look telling him he was ready and the two got up from the couch to leave Mr. Oliver with the other officers in the room.

Christopher met them on the way back out through the front door and tapped Sean on the shoulder. "There was an empty bottle of wine in the trash with a clean glass next to the sink. Looks like she was doing a little boozing and watching T.V. The killer would have had a clear view of her from that window."

As they walked outside, they could see Mark's guys loading Janet Oliver into the back of the coroner's truck. Christopher's team met them at the door and filled them in on what they found. "We had more shoe prints outside of the master bedroom. Size ten like the others. We figured we'd check the garage just in case, but we didn't find anything. A couple of guys walked up and down the street. This was the only house with the hose turned on."

Christopher thanked the men and walked down the driveway. Dave turned over to Sean and said, "Do you think he planned this one?"

Sean shook his head. "He hit two different houses earlier in the week. I think he's just sneaking around the neighborhood and peeping windows. When he finds what he wants he turns the hose on."

"That could be. This is easier for him. He doesn't have to work around his victims' schedules when he baits them out of the house." Dave sighed. "The press is going to eat us alive."

Sean and Dave watched the coroner's truck pull away. They knew they were in for long twenty-four hours.

The detectives had another night taken up talking to the victim's neighbors. As they expected, they were unable to find a witness. Dealing with the most recent homicide stole their time and forced them to miss their early morning with the veteran from Vincinni's list.

The day after the murder they held another press conference and received painful questions from desperate reporters. Ed Donaldson didn't hold anything back. The tension in the room was uncomfortable to sit in, let alone speak to. Sean and Dave followed it with another dead-end meeting with Christopher and Mark. The entire team felt frustrated. To add on to their suspicion of the

Garage Killer, Mark was able to confirm that the same type of knife used in the previous homicides had been used in the newest one.

The news was numbing. The killer had done it again and they were tired of being behind the man. They were willing to try anything to get a jump on his next move. The community was under intense pressure but somehow, it still wasn't enough to flush him out.

Calls flooded the station about watchful eyes and dirty looks. Riverwood fell into hysteria. Sean rolled by the Olivers' home the night following the murder, hoping to see another silhouette stalking the streets, but the figure never appeared.

Without answers, the detectives worked through the rest of the week and into a sleepless weekend. They were frustrated and tired, but they had big plans for Monday. They decided it was time to plan another morning with Vincinni's veteran. The welder was their last-ditch hope and their only person of interest whose name they had come across from something that felt like actual police work.

For Sean, the guilt that came with the ongoing crime spree was beginning to make him feel personally responsible for the murders. No matter what he did it never felt like enough, but Monday morning was his shot at redemption.

Chapter 12

All cold cases in Riverwood go to die at the same place, the evidence warehouse. Once enough time has passed and the leads fade away, they're moved to make room for more at the station. A large old bricked garage blends into its surroundings and keeps the memories of forgotten cases that never found redemption.

Jake and Spears had pulled up to the building and removed the lock on the roll-up door. They had come to find out if the bloodied clothing from the Garage Guerrilla cases still existed. Being from a time before DNA testing, it wasn't odd for officers to clean up parts of a crime scene that years later would become the focus of the investigation. Even though the autopsy reports on the three violent murders called out one blood type, there was still a chance that the killer's blood was crusted onto his victims' clothing. The crimes were too violent for there not to have been some form of a struggle.

The two made their way through the building and meandered down rows of neatly filed boxes until they came to a heavily dusted section. Spears spotted one of the cases first and said, "Here, I got one. It's the box from the Oliver murder."

He walked over and slid it off the shelf. Dust peppered the air. Breathing through the chalk-like cloud, Jake came over and watched him lift the lid off to the box. Sure enough, rolled inside was a paper bag that appeared to be wrapped around bloodied clothing. The bag had a dark dried rust color from the blood that had soaked through it. Jake saw the bag and excitedly called out to Spears, "Think that will work?"

"To be honest kid," the captain replied, "I don't know. That's a question for the lab."

They put the lid back on and moved the box to the side. Walking a few more rows down, Jake pulled out another.

"Here," he said, coughing as dust fell around him. "This one is the Philips box."

He slid the box onto the ground and lifted off the lid. Underneath was another rusted bag holding more blood crusted clothes. Spears smiled approvingly and said, "Let's find the last one."

Jake looked back up at the shelves until he spotted it. He called out, "There. It's the Sandoval murder."

The box made a thud as Jake let it hit the ground. He

worked the lid off and looked inside. The last rusted bag laid on top. Jake looked up at Spears. The captain nodded, "This is it. This is what we need. This is our chance for redundancy."

Jake smiled. "Now we know we're not wasting the old man's time."

He put the lid back on the box and slid it next to the other ones by Spears. Jake asked, "What do we do next?"

"We go to the lab."

Traffic was light on the highway. It took thirty minutes to get to the county forensics lab. Spears pulled up in front of the building and put his hazards on. He didn't have time to park. They had loaded the evidence boxes in the back seat behind them. Each box carried the same piece of optimism. Bloodied clothing from the three up close and personal knife murders attributed to the Garage Guerrilla. The names and dates on the boxes were Kathrine Sandoval, killed on April 7, 1969, Helen Philips, murdered on May 29, 1969, and Janet Oliver, knifed down on July 9, 1969.

Their unidentified killer was still only known through the decades by his notorious pseudonym. Jake and Spears felt compelled to change that. His blood, if there was any, was the way to his name. The two men were eager to extract a DNA profile and get the information into CODIS. Jake had confidence from the idea that even if they didn't get a hit from the national database, they could still pursue GEDmatch. Between the two systems, they were going to find their man, but first, they needed his blood.

Inside they met with a woman Spears had talked to on the phone. Rachel Wood was in charge of all forensic DNA testing for the county. A veteran in her field, she had seen her fair share of cold cases. She met Jake and Spears in the lobby of the building and quickly introduced herself. She appeared hesitant about the idea Spears had proposed on the phone. She knew how difficult the task would be and she felt it was up to her to bring the two men up to speed on reality. She held a firm expression that turned into firm words. "Is this what we talked about?" She was pointing at the boxes they were carrying in.

Spears set down his box and nodded. "Yes, Ma'am. All three cases we spoke about on the phone." Spears lifted the lid to the box he brought in and exposed the bagged-up clothing.

Rachel examined the bag. "Do we have any reference DNA from the victims' families?"

"For right now, no. We're strictly looking for a link between these cases. If you're able to pull a profile from one that matches what you find on another, that's all we're hoping for."

Jake set down his two boxes and smiled at her.

"Thank you."

Rachel quickly snapped back, "Don't be thanking me yet. You said this was 50-year-old dried blood. Dried blood that's been sitting in a temperamental climate only protected by a paper bag. I've never worked with something this old."

Jake's stomach knotted up and his smile went away. Spears stole her attention back by asking, "You've gotten DNA out of dried blood before, haven't you?"

Rachel sighed, "Yes, but unwatched samples have the possibility of growing microbes that can dilute the DNA."

Neither of them responded. Jake and Spears were over their head as far as how the actual science came together. All Jake knew about the subject was what he could find online. Rachel could see the change in their faces. Feeling that she had kicked their hopes down a little too much she added some assurances to the conversation and said, "However, from what you've told me, we didn't have these samples exposed to light and that's the biggest issue. Dried blood can be volatile, but it is one of the best ways to preserve DNA. If your blood samples never experienced extreme microbial growths, then we should be able to produce something here."

Jake felt relieved. He'd worried Rachel was going to shut them down right there in the lobby. He learned his lesson from his first thank you and instead only smiled.

Rachel picked up one of the boxes and said, "I'll call you when we get the results."

A restless few days passed for Jake. The test results were all he could think about. In his wait, he spent most of his time rereading the Garage Guerrilla articles and looking up the Golden State Killer case again. New articles had come out detailing the case in California and Jake had read every one of them. Spears had gotten used to giving him a hard time for being glued to a computer screen or his phone. He could see the obsession in the young man. For the most part, he let him go down the rabbit hole. Spears wasn't going to involve Jake in more cold cases, and he didn't want to turn him over to Julie until after they heard some news from the lab. He wanted to keep their focus on the Garage Guerrilla.

The week pushed into Friday and the sleepy station was at work with business as usual. Jake was scrolling through articles on his phone when one made him jump out of his chair. He ran over to Spears and yelled, "They got another one!"

The captain squinted back at him. "Who?"

Jake handed Spears his phone. The captain looked down at *The Seattle Times* article. It detailed the arrest of a 55-year-old man linked to a double murder from 1987. It stated that investigators used the same methods as the team that brought in the Golden State Killer. Jake spoke to him as he read. "I knew someone else would do it!"

Spears was impressed. He agreed with Jake on how monumental the case in California had been and reading about another dead-end case finding its way through GEDmatch reinforced his optimism. If they could get a DNA profile belonging to the Garage Guerrilla, their first move would still be CODIS, but having more confirmation that GEDmatch could work successfully was reassuring.

The captain handed Jake his phone back. "That call from Rachel can't come soon enough."

Jake laughed. "You don't have to tell me. It's the only thing on my mind."

"It may be next week, but don't worry kid. She'll call."

Monday came as the anticipation rolled into a new week. The day had slowly moved into the late morning when Spears's phone rang. He picked it up calmly and answered, "Captain Spears."

He immediately recognized Rachel's voice.

"Captain, we've concluded our testing."

Spears could feel a tinge of nervousness. He realized he had become attached to the results.

"Unfortunately," Rachel continued, "we were only able to detect one DNA profile on the clothing from the Oliver and Philips cases."

"What about the Sandoval case?"

As Spears talked, Jake overheard him and made his way over. Rachel replied, "Well sir, we got lucky on that one. We discovered DNA from two individuals on the victim's clothing."

The news hit like a punch. Spears couldn't believe it. Jake couldn't hear Rachel on the phone, but he could see the captain's reaction. He yelled out at Spears, "What's she saying? Put it on speaker."

Spears hushed him with a hand. He was too focused to pull the phone away. Rachel went on. "It was easy to tell why the old coroner's report only listed one blood type. The two individuals shared the same — A positive."

Spears hadn't even thought of checking for that after learning the killer's blood type. The captain replied, "Great work, Rachel. I can't believe you actually got something. I'll talk it over here with Jake and we'll get back to you."

Jake was impatiently listening to Spears, dying to be filled in. The captain hung up the phone and smiled back at Jake. "Now, we can't get ahead of ourselves."

Jake enthusiastically replied, "*What do you mean* we can't get ahead of ourselves? She got him!"

"Potentially. She was only able to get another DNA profile out of the Sandoval case. She had nothing on the Oliver or Philips cases. Which means we don't have exactly what we need."

Jake understood Spears and replied, "No redundancy. Right."

The captain nodded.

Jake found a chair and took a seat while the information set in. Spears spoke as he sat down. "There's only one more piece to the puzzle that we haven't checked."

Jake thought about it, then looked back at the captain. "Amber Ridge."

"Exactly. Kennedy said the killer had been cut that night too."

Jake remembered the rest of the story and reminded Spears. "But he also said the coroner didn't find another blood type."

"That's true, but that was almost 50 years ago. Our tests are far more accurate now. Being such a violent murder, there could've been just an overwhelming amount of the victim's blood, or maybe they shared the same blood type again. Either way, we have a phone call to make."

Jake didn't waste any time. He pulled out his phone and looked up the number to the Amber Ridge police station. Spears watched him from across his desk as Jake dialed the number and put the phone on speaker. The call connected quickly, and a young man spoke to them.

"Amber Ridge Police. How can I help you?"

Jake talked into the phone. "Hello, my name is Detective Jake Caldwell with the Riverwood Police. I'm following a cold case that involves a case from your jurisdiction. Do you have anyone I can talk to?"

"Just a second."

The phone went silent for a while until someone picked up the line. "This is Sergeant Adams, what can I do for you?"

"Sergeant, I'm Detective Jake Caldwell with the Riverwood Police. We've been looking into multiple cold cases from 1969 and we have reason to believe some of our cases are connected to a homicide that occurred in your city. Have you ever heard of the killer called the Garage Guerrilla?

The sergeant responded confidently, "Nope. Never heard of him."

"Well sir, one of his alleged cases happened in Amber Ridge and we believe that case carries significant DNA evidence if you still have it around."

"You said 1969? Do you have the case number, date, or a victim name?"

"Unfortunately, no. All we have is a description of the case."

The sergeant sighed, "That makes it tough, but we still may be able to find it. What do you got?"

Jake tried his best to sum it up. "It would have happened sometime in either June or July of '69. The case was a single homicide, a woman stabbed outside her home. The crime happened at night and her garden hose would've been running."

There was a pause over the line. Jake could hear Sergeant Adams writing down the details. He was happy the man seemed so willing to help. The sergeant replied, "That'll do. We'll see what we can do for you. I'll have someone look into this and we'll give you a call when we got some news. Shouldn't take too long."

"I appreciate that sergeant. It'll be a big help."

After Jake hung up the phone, he immediately became anxious about having to spend more time waiting. From the conversation Spears had with Rachel, they seemed so close to getting answers. They were one case away from confirming the Garage Guerrilla's DNA, but if Amber Ridge didn't have the case they needed, they'd be out of luck. Jake just wanted some answers already. The anticipation was starting to take a toll on him.

The young detective was back at his desk, close to finishing his coffee. As the liquid inched lower, he nervously began to chew on the Styrofoam cup's edge. The angst he had from waiting for the phone call from Amber Ridge wasn't something he enjoyed. It had been close to an hour since he had spoken to Sergeant Adams and he was growing impatient.

Jake had forgotten to ask the man about a timeframe on when he could expect a callback and was contemplating reaching out to him again when his phone rang. He let it ring once before picking up.

"Detective Caldwell, It's Sergeant Adams. I believe we found your cold case."

Jake instantly felt a weight off his shoulders. They still had a chance. The sergeant went on. "A woman named Anna Schneider was stabbed to death outside of her home on the night of June 4, 1969."

Jake didn't even have to look at the file. He knew the sergeant was right. It matched the description and timeline perfectly. Jake replied to Adams, "That sounds like it. Do you guys still have the evidence? I'm looking specifically for her clothing."

"You're in luck, my man. Clothing, shoes and all of the photographs are still in storage."

Jake felt a chill run down his back. Getting Spears his redundancy was possible again. He eagerly replied, "Sergeant, do you mind if we come down and check it out?"

"No one's touched it in decades. It's all yours."

"When's the soonest you can meet with us?"

The sergeant paused for a bit to check his calendar. "Today, if you absolutely need it. Otherwise, we can set up some time this week."

"Today would be best. Where should we meet you?"

Adams replied, "How about our warehouse in around an hour? It's pretty close to our station. I can text you the address."

Jake agreed and ended the conversation. After he hung up, he rushed over to Spears and said, "Amber Ridge just called. They confirmed our case and gave us the green light to head down and check it out."

Spears looked up from his computer. "What time?"

"In an hour."

The captain didn't need to hear anything else. He shut down his computer and grabbed his things. "It'll take us longer in traffic. Let's go."

The Amber Ridge evidence warehouse looked newer than the one they had in Riverwood. It was an aluminum building that resembled something that might hold a boat, not cold cases. Spears and Jake got there early and sat in their car waiting for the Amber Ridge PD to show up. Jake nervously chewed on his fingernails as he scanned the horizon.

After a few minutes, a police car came around the corner. Jake got out and waved to it. Two people got out of the car and walked over towards him. One of them asked, "Detective Caldwell?"

"Yeah, that's me."

The older officer reached out his hand. "I'm Sergeant Adams. We got your cold case file and should have the evidence still in there somewhere."

He handed Jake the case in his other hand. Jake walked the file over and put it on the hood of Spears's car to quickly skim through it. Sure enough, it was just how Kennedy had described it. He flipped through photographs and then over to the autopsy report where he looked for blood types. The victim's blood, listed as O positive, was the only blood found. He flipped the file back over and closed it.

Jake looked back at the other officers and said, "Thank you. This is huge for us."

Adams nodded, "Of course. We only had a dozen or so cases from 1969 so it wasn't that hard to find."

The sergeant led them over to a side door of the building and unlocked it. The small group walked inside. The warehouse had the same smell as the one in Riverwood, dust and old file boxes. It gave Jake a similar feeling, too, like a void space always in a constant state of waiting.

The group weaved their way almost to the back of the warehouse guided by a year system. They stopped at a dusty rack. The sergeant began to scan the boxes until he said, "Here it is. The Anna Schneider case, June 4, 1969."

He pulled the box from its purgatory and set it on

the ground. Wiggling off the lid he revealed what was inside. Jake felt his heart beating faster. He kept his hopes high and let himself look in. Much like the Riverwood boxes, a paper bag sat on top. Adams pulled it out and held it up. The bag was stuck to the clothing in parts and through an opening, they could see dried blood coating the fabric. Sergeant Adams asked, "Is this what you're after?"

Spears nodded, "Yes, sir."

Adams put the bag back in the box and slid it over to Jake. "I hope this helps tie together your cold cases, gentlemen. It hasn't done us any favors in the last 50 years."

Jake looked down at the box as if it were buried treasure and said, "We think it will. We appreciate the help, guys."

Jake and Spears walked their new evidence out to the car. Jake slid the box behind the passenger seat and they both got in. After Spears started the car, he looked over at Jake to say, "This is our last shot. It's all up to Rachel."

Jake's nerves came back to him. He could feel his stomach knotting up again. He just wanted to know the results already. Spears put the car in drive, and they went on their way to the lab.

For the majority of the drive, they were silent. Jake had been busy dealing with excitement while trying to fight off his own doubts. Spears had made him phone

Rachel before they arrived. As they pulled up to the crime lab, she was outside, arms crossed and waiting. Neither man wanted to let her down. Jake prayed that the clothes in the box behind him had the blood they needed.

Flashes stirred in his imagination of what he would become if it panned out that they'd run into a dead-end. He was too invested now. If they failed, perhaps it would be the beginning of his end. He'd soon find himself like Sean Kennedy, an old man with boxes of evidence in his basement, spending Sunday mornings in retirement reviewing old police work instead of going to the golf course. If this was his first case, how many more would he have?

Jake pushed those thoughts aside and got out of the car. Rachel called out to them, "I'm impressed you're back so quickly. It's rare to get something new on a case this old."

Spears had fished the box out of the car and held it in his hand. "We got lucky," he replied. "An old detective pointed us in the right direction."

Rachel walked over and took the box from the captain. She then told them, "You know how this goes. It might take a little bit, but we'll make sure it gets a thorough test. I'll try to get this in the rotation as soon as I can. Now I'm curious if you guys got something." Rachel took the box and disappeared into the lab.

Wednesday morning, two days later, Jake hovered around the break room. In the last few weeks, he had drunk more coffee than he was comfortable admitting. A move he'd picked up from Spears. The caffeine gave him jittery fingers, but it was his anxious anticipation that bothered him the most.

At the moment he was taking up his time by chewing through his latest Styrofoam cup and walking back and forth between the breakroom and the bullpen. After being glued to his phone for so long he had a headache and couldn't sit still. He wasn't sure if Rachel would call him or Spears, so he liked being on his feet in case he heard the captain's phone ring. He was on his way back to the break room, thinking about getting a fresh cup when he heard Spears's phone. The sound stopped him in his tracks. He waited and listened. He heard Spears pick it up and answer, "Captain Spears."

Jake was too far away to hear the person on the other line, but he knew he could figure out the phone call from the captain's reaction. He heard Spears reply, "Really?"

Jake waited for more. Whoever was on the other end was doing most of the talking. Spears replied again, "That's insane. I can't believe it! This is wonderful news."

Jake felt a rush of excitement. He couldn't just listen in anymore. He threw his chewed-up cup into the garbage and ran over to the captain's office. He hoped the phone call was the one they had been waiting for. Jake had a good feeling about it and Spears's face said it all. The man was beaming. The captain finished up by saying, "Thanks, Rachel. Yes, CODIS is the next step. Ok, will do. I'll talk to you soon."

Spears hung up the phone and looked at Jake. He didn't even have to say anything. Jake was so excited he practically yelled at him, "No way!"

Spears laughed, "Yeah, she did it. She got a match between the Sandoval case and the one from Amber Ridge."

Jake threw his hands in the air. He wanted to scream. Spears tried to calm him down and said, "Alright, alright. I know. It's crazy news, but it's not over yet."

Jake took a breath and tried to compose himself. Spears put his hands together and said, "Now we really have to cross our fingers, because she's about to load it up into CODIS."

Chapter 13

1969

It was an hour before sunrise and the morning was cool and peaceful. Sean and Dave sat in a cigarette-marinated car with the radio low, sipping coffee. Being a Monday after a work-filled weekend, they were too tired to talk and too overwhelmed to have anything to chat about. Their car was parked just on the other side of a large metal fence that surrounded an active construction site. It was the job site where the last veteran Vincinni flagged as a person of interest happened to work.

Jason Harper had an athletic build and a quick temper. He stood 5'10" with black hair and a size ten shoe. His blood type also happened to be A positive. After a dishonorable discharge at the age of nineteen, he had paved an interesting life for himself. His bad behavior got him out of Vietnam, but it also put him in and out of prison and jails. He couldn't stay straight even when he was paid to. He was known to frequent the red-light district and gentlemen's clubs. Even though It was illegal for him to own a gun, the detectives assumed he had one but knew that he wouldn't be armed at work.

Sean and Dave were well aware of the man's reputation and, given the most recent murder, they decided it was time to surprise him. All they needed was a couple of seconds to stare him in the face, ask him some questions and check out his right hand. Sean was pounding the coffee. They both were on the verge of madness and they had exhausted all of their efforts in the past week. Without enough sleep and fueled only by cigarettes and caffeine, the two had disintegrated into shells of themselves.

A song came on the radio and brought Dave to life. "Hey, Johnny Cash. Now we're talking."

He turned the radio up and pulled out another cigarette. Sean was halfway through his coffee thermos and had to take a piss. He got out of the car and walked by the fence. It was still too dark to see beyond a block's distance, but the sky was beginning to turn orange in the east. Cars were trickling in and parking nearby. Men with hard hats got out of them and filed through the gate into the job site.

Sean got back in the car and turned off Dave's radio. Dave angrily snapped at him, "What the hell?"

Sean pointed at the men going through the gate. They both knew it was getting close to go-time, but they still had to figure out where Jason would be on the job site. They knew they couldn't just wander around without standing out. The detectives needed to do everything they could to maintain their element of surprise, otherwise, they risked their man getting away if he had something to hide. Sean and Dave hoped they could pass through the job site unnoticed until they could speak with Jason's boss. They didn't want to talk to any of his colleagues. Shaking down a fellow employee to point out one of their own usually wasn't a crowd-pleaser, but they'd have to try it if they had no other option.

The detectives waited a few minutes more and watched the last of the men enter the job site. It wasn't long before a foreman barked orders and people began to disperse.

Dave looked over at Sean and they both got out of the car. Dave confidently led the way. Sean followed as he strolled up to the open gate and walked through it. They had a rough description of their man but picking him out from the other guys would be next to impossible.

Five steps in, a bearded man in overalls stepped in front of them. "Can I help you guys?"

Sean and Dave knew they weren't going to get far, they were the only guys around wearing slacks. Dave couldn't tell if the man in front of him was the one in charge. He asked, "Are you the boss around here?"

The bearded man replied, "Yeah, one of them."

Dave took a chance and quickly flashed his badge to explain why they were there. "We're looking for Jason Harper. You know him?"

The man stroked his beard and shook his head. "No, I don't, but I know the man who does. The superintendent is just around the corner."

The man was pointing at large concrete forms. Dave thanked him and they walked around the forms. There the detectives saw another man bending over building plans. Dave walked up to him and got his attention. The superintendent turned and looked at them with questioning eyes. "Who are you?"

Dave pulled out his badge, introduced Sean and himself and talked honestly. "Morning sir, We're not here for any trouble. We're detectives with the Riverwood Police. We're following a homicide investigation and we believe one of your workers, Jason Harper, may have vital information regarding the case. Do you mind if we speak with him?"

The superintendent looked Sean and Dave up and down. He studied them awhile before nodding. "Yeah, he should be here today," he replied. "I got him on the second floor."

Dave put his hands together in a thank you. "We appreciate that. Would you mind showing him to us?"

The superintendent put his things down and walked past the detectives. "He's this way. Come on."

Sean and Dave followed after him. He led them around more concrete forms and up a flight of stairs. The detectives stayed close behind him and kept their eyes out for loose nails and wooden planks. They turned a corner and passed the bearded man they spoke to before. Sean gave the man a friendly nod, but he only made eye contact with Dave and continued walking in the other way. His face was cold and tense. His demeanor made Sean feel uneasy. Their guide turned back to them and called out, "He's right over here."

Sean took his mind off of the bearded man and followed along. They took a right around one more wall and saw a worker sprinting in the other direction. Welding equipment was laying on the floor where he had been. Sean immediately realized what the bearded man had just done and took off after the running man who he assumed to be Jason Harper. Dave yelled, "Shit!" and ran after him.

They blew past the superintendent in pursuit. The detectives ran down the open hall and turned the corner where Jason had just disappeared. Sean spotted him again and got into his stride. He began to close in on the man and had caught up to ten yards behind him when Jason jumped into a quick left. Sean followed and yelled, "Stop! Police!"

Jason kept running. He went up a flight of stairs, out of their sight. Sean followed, but when he got to the top of the stairs Jason was gone. He looked around the empty floor and then noticed that Jason must have used the nearby scaffold to get off of the floor. He hurried down the scaffold and caught sight Jason below, dodging between trucks and workers in the laydown yard.

Dave had fallen back and was well behind them. Sean got down to the dirt and tried his best not to lose his footing as he ran through the job site. Once more he began to gain on him, but Jason jumped up on a concrete form and climb to the top. Sean got to the base of the forms and started up them. He worked his way up to the top expecting a fight but when he pulled himself over the edge Jason wasn't there. The forms were backed up to the fence surrounding the job site. Sean could see that Jason had jumped off of them. He was now running in the street past parked cars. Sean knew that if he followed him, Jason would still get to his car before Sean could stop him. He watched the man until he got into a truck and drove away.

Dave made it to the base of the concrete forms and called out to Sean, "You alright?"

"I'm fine. He just drove off in a blue and white Ford pickup."

Sean climbed down and met Dave. In between hard breaths he said, "We need to radio this in. Vincinni should have his last known address, maybe we can meet him at home."

They could feel the eyes of the watching construction site on them. Dave jogged off to get to the car while Sean caught his breath and walked through the gathering crowd. As Sean made it out to the street Dave pulled the car up. He got inside and Dave hit the gas. "I got patrol cars out looking for a blue and white Ford. Vincinni's getting us the address."

Dave screeched the tires to a halt in front of the address Vincinni gave them over the radio. They eyed the house from inside the car and scanned the street for the blue and white Ford. They couldn't see one and the house looked dead. The detectives wanted to wait until they had more boots on the ground before they approached the home. They both knew that if they were, in fact, sitting outside the house that belonged to their infamous garage killer, going up to the door by themselves could be a death sentence. Given Jason Harper's reputation, they would be undoubtedly walking into a firefight.

Sirens became recognizable in the distance. Their backup was almost there. Sean and Dave checked their pistols and got out of the car. Two patrol cars came into view and burned down the street in their direction. Sean waved them down as they got close and they parked behind Dave's car. Lieutenant Harrison got out of the front car and called out to Sean, "Do you really think it's him?"

"He knew who we were, and he ran. We didn't even get a word in with him."

Harrison nodded and looked back at the other officers to say, "We're going to knock on the door. I need a guy on either side of the house. If he runs, you follow."

The officers jogged up to the house and cautiously took their places. Each of them carefully scanned the windows, looking for an opening someone inside could shoot at them from.

Harrison led Sean and Dave up to the house. He made it up the small front steps and quickly moved over the porch. The lieutenant stood to the side of the door and rapped on its metal screen. He yelled, "Jason Harper. This is the Riverwood Police."

They all waited for a sound from inside the house but heard nothing. Harrison looked back at the detectives and put his hand over the pistol on his hip. He opened the screen door and moved over to the other side. There he knocked on the wood door itself. This time much louder. "Jason Harper. This is the Riverwood Police."

Again, they waited for a sound, but it never came. Sean and Dave were watching the window blinds for movement. Dave whispered to Harrison, "Is the door unlocked?"

The lieutenant turned back to him and said, "Do we know he's inside?"

"No, but he could've beat us here and he could be

destroying evidence. Don't you think we should go in?"

Harrison looked back at the door and thought about it. He moved his hand towards the handle, but Sean stopped him by saying, "Do we know for sure whether this is the right address?"

Harrison looked back at him, wide-eyed. "Do we?"

Sean shook his head. "I don't think so. This was the address on his parole report, but we don't know if it's been confirmed. I don't see a blue and white Ford anywhere."

Harrison sighed heavily. He still had his hand near the door handle. Sean continued. "The house isn't going anywhere. I still think he's on the road. I say we keep a patrol car here and get back on the highways. We can confirm this as his address and come back."

Harrison was torn, his hand still hovering over the door handle. He looked back at Dave and pulled his hand away. "Sean's right. Let's keep an eye on this place and get back to the road. If he shows up here, we'll know."

The lieutenant turned and walked back off the porch. He called out for the other officers and let them in on the plan. Dave looked over at Sean unsure whether they'd made the right decision, but he kept his mouth shut. The detectives walked back to the car and holstered their guns. Sean stared at the house from the street before he got back in the car. If they were making a mistake by leaving, then he was willing to take that chance. There was no way Jason Harper could get in or out of the house unseen. The more eyes they had on the road, the better.

The detectives got in the car and tuned into the chatter on the police radio. Dave put the car into drive, and they began exploring the neighborhood. The radio sounded off nonstop as the patrols Dave asked for earlier coordinated their tight watch on the city's major exits. Dave drove down the streets adjacent to the one they had just been parked on and the detectives kept a close eye out for Harper's pickup. As they meandered around the neighborhood a frantic voice came over the radio. "I've got something here!" Sean turned the radio up. "I have a blue and white Ford going westbound on Sixth Avenue past Kipling Street."

Sixth Avenue led out towards the crime lab and intersected with the highway that cut into the mountains. They needed to stop him before he got on that highway. Sean picked up the radio and said, "Pull him over but don't get out of the car until you have back up. We're ten minutes out."

Dave frantically turned the car around and headed for Sixth Avenue.

As Dave got behind the cruiser on the side of the road, Sean got a good look at the truck parked in front of it. "That could be him," he told Dave. His voice carried with excitement.

He quickly got out of the car and so did the officer in front of him. Sean hurried over to him and yelled out, "Has he tried anything?"

"No. He's just been waiting."

Sean looked back out to the truck and watched it. He couldn't make out the man inside, but he could see that he was looking at him through his rearview mirror. Sean looked back at the officer. "You approach the driver side. I'll take the passenger side. Don't get ahead of me."

Sean drew his pistol and started for the truck. The officer followed after Sean and pulled out his pistol. Dave watched them moving and stayed in his car in case Jason sped off. As the officer approached the driver's side of the truck the man rolled down his window. Sean yelled out to him, "No, no!"

The driver cried out from inside. "Please, don't shoot! I don't know what I did."

The voice sounded desperate and scared. Sean no longer felt threatened and ran up to the passenger side of the car. He looked through the window and saw a man sweating profusely and trembling. Was this Jason Harper? He had black hair and looked to be the right size. His hands were shaking over his head and his eyes were wild with fear. The officer got to his window and asked for his license. The man nervously fumbled for it and gave it to him. The officer read the name out to Sean. "His name is Greg Sutter."

Sean knew it couldn't have been Jason the second he heard his voice. His shoulders dropped and he closed his eyes. He replied back to the officer, "Let him go."

He holstered his gun and turned back for the car. Dave could tell from Sean's body language that it wasn't Jason. As Sean got to the car Dave reached over and rolled down his window. "Not our guy?"

Sean didn't respond and got in the car. He rubbed his hands over his face and muffled, "Where the hell could he go?"

Sean and Dave drove back to the station. On their way, they listened to other patrol cars radioing in traffic stops with blue and white Fords. Again, and again, it was innocent men. The truck was a popular vehicle for the area, so the police had their hands full.

The detectives figured they would let the other officers handle the roads. Their time was better spent gathering more information about Jason Harper. Once they did get him in, they would need to pull together enough evidence to prove he was the Garage Killer. As it stood, they didn't have anything incriminating on him tied to the murders. They only had him fleeing an officer.

When the detectives walked through the doors of the station, they headed straight for Vincinni. He hovered over a radio with detective Hull, listening to the traffic stops. Once he noticed Sean and Dave he perked up.

Sean spoke to him, "We left a car at the house, but we didn't see anything. Can you confirm that it's his address and get us a warrant?"

Vincinni nodded. Dave wasn't entirely sure what Sean had up his sleeve. He followed him back over to their desks. Sean took a seat and picked up Jason Harper's criminal record. Dave was confused to see Sean sit down. He asked, "What are we doing here, Sean?"

His partner waved him off and rubbed his forehead. "I'm trying to think. Once we get him here, we need something to tie him to the case. Right now, all we know for sure is that he's an idiot."

"It won't be in his paperwork. Let's go back to his job site. His boss can tell us when he was at work and when he wasn't. We can try to build a timeline."

Sean hadn't even thought of going back to the job site, but he knew Dave was right, he wouldn't find anything in the station. He looked up at Dave and got out of his chair. "Let's go."

The detectives parked their car in front of the job site. Dave got out and led the way through the gate again. This time they walked right over to where they met the superintendent earlier in the morning. As they turned the corner around the concrete forms the man wasn't there. Sean and Dave walked over to the building plans that he was reading before and waited.

Soon after, the superintendent returned. Once he saw Sean and Dave he sighed. He knew he'd have to speak to the detectives again. Dave started the conversation. "Got anywhere we can talk?"

The superintendent looked over at a small trailer and pointed. "Let's go in there."

Sean and Dave followed him into the metal trailer. Inside he had a desk and file cabinets set up. He moved behind the desk and took a seat in his chair. Sean got right to business. "When you hired Jason Harper, were you aware of his record?"

The man shuffled in his seat. "Yes, but we were out of options and I needed a welder."

"Well, obviously this has escalated to more than just us needing a few words with him."

"What do you need from me?"

Dave answered for Sean. "Did he ever give you any reasons for concern? Was he a problem?"

The superintendent folded his arms. "Sure. He was a cocky guy with a bad attitude. I didn't like dealing with him too much, but I needed him around."

Sean pulled out a notebook and began to write. He asked, "What about his timecards. Were there ever days he didn't show?"

"Yeah, he bailed on us a couple of times." The superintendent reached down and pulled out a drawer. "Here are the timecards."

He threw them on the table and started going through them for Jason's. After he picked a few out he showed them to the detectives and said, "He's made it every day for the last two weeks, but he had some spotty weeks before that, if I remember right."

Janet Oliver's murder was only the week before. The timecards didn't give them enough information. Sean and Dave could see that the only way they could build Jason's timeline was by speaking with him directly.

Dave replied to the superintendent, "Would you happen to know anything about where he would've gone?"

The man shook his head and Sean asked him another question. "Was he ever violent on the job or did he ever come in injured?

"Not that I can recall."

Sean got more specific. "What about his right hand? Was it ever injured?"

"He wears gloves. If his hand was messed up it didn't interfere with his work."

Dave realized they weren't going to hear what they wanted to and ended the conversation after handing the superintendent his card. "Well, if you can think of any valuable information please don't hesitate to call."

The superintendent nodded and got up to show the detectives out. The man had been less than helpful, but Sean and Dave had gotten used to low expectations. They walked off the job site and got back into their car, nowhere closer to answers than they had been at the start of the day. If they couldn't find Jason Harper it was going to be a rough road ahead.

The next day, Jason was still on the run. Sean and Dave went back to his house and barged in with a warrant. Inside they only found empty beer cans and rotted food. The man had most likely escaped the city. Their warrant didn't produce anything useful and they were left to a manhunt without a lead.

Time flew by quickly and it took two weeks before the detectives had an update. They were contacted by another police force in Texas who claimed they had Jason Harper. Sean and Dave were excited to hear the news. Somehow, he had slipped out of Riverwood and found his way to El Paso. There he held up a convenience store and was arrested after attempting to flee. As Sean and Dave spoke to the other officers their excitement faded away. It turned out that Jason ran from them because he had been robbing homes around Riverwood and thought that someone had finally ratted him out. Worst of all, they were forced to rule him out as a suspect once they learned that he didn't have the scar on his right hand from the encounter with Tracy Vanderbelt.

Time became even more of a blur and three weeks quickly passed without an update in the case. It had been weeks since the last murder, but the calls never slowed down. The citizens of Riverwood were still running up the station's switchboard with reports of suspicious activity and running hoses. Chief Perry did what he could to keep the helicopter out on rotations, but the city was running out of funds. Night patrols continued to be scheduled and the detectives had them sweep the areas with the most calls. Yet, even with all the noise, the case was at a standstill and the detectives were now joining the searches around the city at night. They waited out their weeks as just another car on patrol.

On a warm night in the last week of August, Dave was behind the wheel. The summer streets of Riverwood were full of people. Dog walkers, kids, and cars occupied the city into the late hours, making it hard to spot someone doing something out of the ordinary. Dave was driving Sean and him in and out of streets around the ditch trail when he made a familiar turn. He pulled the car over to the side of the road and parked in front of 1722 Shoshone, the former home of Abigail Thompson. A "For Sale" sign still stood on the front lawn. Sean looked over at Dave and asked, "What are we doing here?"

Dave stared at the dark house. His memory took him back to their first night on the case. He replied, "Why did it start here? What was it about her that caught his attention?"

"Vulnerability? She was alone."

Dave shook his head, still staring across the street. "That could be. Or, was it something else?"

"Attraction?"

Dave nodded. "Sure. I guess we could call it that. He wasn't just after the helpless. If he was, we would've been responding to dead prostitutes and outcasts. These women weren't that."

Sean pulled out a cigarette and stared down the street. He lit the end and put his head back while closing his eyes. Dave continued to stare at the house, hoping that in time it would give him some closure, but nothing came to him. He still felt as exhausted and defeated as he had in the weeks before. Sean took a few drags of his cigarette and broke the silence. "I came back here the night after it happened." He paused and blew out the smoke. "I was just trying to clear my head after that day we had, and I parked right here. Just like this. I killed the lights and was watching the house when I saw something."

Dave turned and looked at him. "In the house?"

"No, just beyond that streetlight on the corner."

Sean opened his eyes and pointed at the dimly lit corner. Dave looked over at it and asked, "What was it?"

Sean went on. "It was a guy. He had stopped on the corner and was staring back at me. It only lasted a couple of seconds. He stared at me and then he ran."

Sean squinted back at the streetlight remembering

the snowy night. "I drove over there but all I found were his prints in the snow." He looked over at Dave. "They led right into the ditch trail."

Dave couldn't believe what he was hearing. He replied, "Jesus, Sean why didn't you tell me sooner?"

Sean put his cigarette back in his mouth. "What would I have said? I drove around looking for the guy, but I didn't even know exactly who it was that I was looking for."

Dave wasn't sure what to think of Sean's story, but he could understand why he'd kept it to himself. Dave asked, "Did you ever go back to any of the other ones?"

"Every one."

"You're kidding me? And did you ever see anything like that again?"

"No, the first time was it."

Dave turned back to the street corner and took a good look at it. Sean watched it with him until Dave replied, "Come on, Let's get out of here. We got other houses to check out. We had two new calls last night."

Chapter 14

The phone rang two times before it connected. Jake was trying to reach Sean Kennedy. Spears had given him the ok to call the old man. They both felt he deserved to know they were actually making headway in the case and not just glossing over the files. They had pulled off a longshot by collecting the Garage Guerrilla's DNA, but he wanted to let Kennedy know they were now going after the impossible. They were going after his name.

Jake could hear static on the other line and spoke first. "Mr. Kennedy? Mr. Kennedy, it's Jake Caldwell with the Riverwood Police."

Sean grunted over the phone. "Hello, Jake. I can hear you."

"Sir, we have some exciting updates for you about the Garage Guerrilla case."

"Oh, that's great news."

"We hooked up with Amber Ridge and found the case you had described at the diner. We were able to test the clothing saved in storage from the knife murders and what we found was astounding. The blood that we collected from Amber Ridge matched blood left behind from one of your cases in Riverwood."

Sean's voice went up a pitch. "You got his *blood*?"

"Yes, sir. We got his DNA."

The line went silent. Jake was about to ask Kennedy if he was still there when the old man came back. "You're kidding me."

Jake smiled and reassured him. "No sir, we actually pulled it off. It turns out his blood has been sitting on that clothing for the last 50 years."

"What can you do with it? You don't have his name, do you?"

"No sir, but that's what we're going for now. We're putting his DNA profile into the national system. If he was ever a blip on police radar in the last twenty years, we'll soon know his name."

Sean knew how the system worked. He had read plenty about it in the paper throughout his years in retirement. Jake went on. "I know you understand we're not allowed to discuss ongoing investigations, but we figured you were an exception. We wanted to fill you in on our progress and let you know that our meeting last week helped tremendously."

"I appreciate it, Jake. I'm very interested to hear what you get next. Thanks for the call."

Jake hung up the phone and sat back satisfied. It felt good to give the old man some positive news, but it also added more stress to the outcome. He desperately wanted the chance to give Sean Kennedy that next call. He had never wanted something so bad in his life but as it stood, his hopes were left to the system. CODIS.

CODIS had worked all over the nation on countless cold cases but it could only rely on missing persons, felons and suspects. Jake knew plenty about CODIS. He was excited about GEDmatch, but he still knew there was a chance CODIS could find their man. He let himself take hold of the idea that perhaps the Garage Guerrilla had moved on to kill elsewhere, got caught and was living a life behind bars. If their man was already rotting in a cell, then CODIS would find him there.

The idea made sense. Psychologists backed the theory that psychopathic killers were unable to avoid their own impulses. Bundy was the perfect example. Yet, even though the theory existed, Jake understood there were always outliers and he also knew that if the Garage Guerrilla had been caught for another crime, it most likely would have been in a world before DNA. The man may have served out a full sentence and the only thing left behind to show for it could be the paperwork.

Without his DNA in the system, he would still be a ghost and CODIS wouldn't find him.

Jake sat at his desk nervously chewing through another Styrofoam cup. In the past week, he had developed a routine of chewing through two a day. If it wasn't for the trash can in his cubicle, he never would have noticed. It was half full of them. Rachel had called them about the blood matching on Wednesday. It was now Friday and Jake couldn't focus on anything else. All he could think about was the next call from Rachel. He walked by Spears's desk every time the captain picked up the phone. His constant wandering made him look crazy.

As the day progressed into lunchtime, the station filled up with the smell of microwaved meals. Jake was starting to think about lunch himself when he heard the captain's phone ring. The sound instantly got him out of his chair. He made his way towards the breakroom to eavesdrop. As he walked into earshot, he heard Spears say what he had been waiting for.

"Rachel. How are you?"

Jake hurried over and peaked his head into Spears's office. The captain waved him in and put the phone on speaker. Rachel came over the line.

"I'm doing good, thanks for asking. I have an update on our DNA project."

Jake had mixed emotions. He had been pacing around Spears's office for the last two days, but now when the call actually came, he couldn't handle the suspense.

Spears replied, "Wonderful. I have Jake in the room here as well."

Rachel cleared her throat. "It was a fantastic effort and I'm still impressed that you found me the evidence to test given the circumstances, but unfortunately we didn't get a hit on CODIS."

Jake's stomach dropped. Spears took the information in and sighed.

"That is unfortunate. We appreciate everything you did for us, Rachel."

Spears sounded as though he was going to end the call, but Jake stared at him with determined eyes, encouraging Spears to remember that they still had a chance. The captain saw Jake's face and knew what he wanted. He caught Rachel before she could reply and said, "There is one other thing we'd like to try. We've never tried this ourselves, but it's getting a lot of attention. Have you heard of GEDmatch?"

Rachel sarcastically laughed, "Yes. I've seen the news."

"Is that a possibility for us?

"I'd have to look more into it. I'm not entirely sure how it's done."

The feeling in Jake's stomach began to ease. She didn't shoot it down. Hope blended back into ambition. Spears looked over at Jake as he spoke into the phone. "Thanks for not saying no."

"If we have the means to use it, then I don't see why not. I'll do some digging and get back to you."

Rachel hung up the phone and left Jake and Spears to wait once more.

The weekend quickly passed and turned into Monday morning. Jake had increasingly become conscious of his nervous habit and brought in a ceramic mug to spare the Styrofoam. He was on his second cup of coffee when his paranoia began to creep in. What if Rachel couldn't do it? They had gotten as far as collecting the offender's DNA and even uploading it into CODIS but tying the blood to the man now hinged on a website. If Rachel couldn't do it, then all of their efforts would boil away and the case would find itself back in the warehouse.

Jake couldn't bear the thought. He decided to focus on other things. He had learned not to torture himself as he had before by listening in on the captain's calls. Instead, he brought headphones and attempted to tune out the sounds of the station while he reviewed the old files once more.

Jake turned up the volume and flipped through the reports and photos of the murders he had been working on for the last month. His plan for a mental escape seemed to be working and he was quickly caught up in rereading the files. The growing angst he hid behind the music felt all but gone until he saw Spears. The captain was standing over him and gesturing him to follow. Jake took his headphones off and followed him. His nerves came back and ate at his stomach, but he confidently walked to Spears's office.

There the captain sat down and pushed a button on his desk phone.

"Ok, Rachel. I got Jake. Go ahead."

Rachel's voice came out of the speaker. "GEDmatch requires an entirely different test then CODIS. CODIS takes what's called STR genotyping while GEDmatch needs SNP genotyping. We'll have to retest our samples."

Spears didn't know what the acronyms meant but he didn't care. He just wanted to know if it could be done. He asked, "Will you be able to do that?"

"I'd have to send it out to a third-party lab, but it can be done. After that, it shouldn't be too complicated. They'll send me a zip file with the SNP information and then it'll be up to you to create a profile on GEDmatch. Once I get it, I can just email you guys the zip file."

"How much is this third-party going to cost, and how soon can it happen?"

"It's pretty affordable. I work with these guys often. They can punch out a test like this in a day or two if I let them know it's important. We already did the hard part of extracting and identifying our samples, I'd just have to get the samples over to them."

Jake and Spears understood what that meant. In a day or two, they could be uploading a profile to GED-match. Spears replied, "Wow. That's a quick turnaround. Let's go for it"

"Glad I could help. This has been exciting. Look out for an email from me in the next couple of days."

Spears ended the conversation and hung up the phone. Jake was ecstatic. He smiled and said, "We actually get to do this."

Spears broke a grin and nodded. "It doesn't feel real yet. I won't believe it until we get it on the website."

Jake fought through another day of waiting, which bled into a second. Wednesday morning arrived. He'd spent his Tuesday watching and reading everything he could find about using GEDmatch. The website seemed complicated, but Jake felt confident that he could upload the zip file and get the profile online. He started his morning off by handling his stress in the way he had become accustomed to. An overdose of caffeine and too many trips to the breakroom. Except this time, he wasn't leaving his cubicle to listen in on the captain's phone calls, he was avoiding his emails.

In the last day, he had checked his email more times

than he had since his first day on the job. Rachel's email
was all he needed to bring the puzzle together and waiting
for it was killing him. As Jake sat back down at his desk
from his latest coffee run, he checked his screen. He had
a new message from Rachel. The title read, "Riverwood
Cold Case Zip." Jake felt a chill go down his spine. It was
here.

He opened the email and saw the zip file. Spears
came around the bullpen and saw Jake at his desk. He
asked, "Did you get the email?"

"Yeah. Come over here. Let's do this."

Jake opened the GEDmatch website and began to
make an account. He spoke to Spears once he opened the
page.

"It wants us to put a name in. What should we do?"

"Let's keep it simple. How about Jake Caldwell?"

Jake typed in his name and email. It took him to a
home page where he clicked on "generic upload." He
filled out his information again and attached the zip file.
The website brought him to a loading page. It processed
the information for thirty seconds until an assigned kit
number flashed on the screen. Jake threw himself back in
his seat and yelled, "It worked! Holy shit, that was fast."

He looked over to Spears who was reading the print
on the finished loading screen. The captain asked,
"What's it say on the bottom there?"

Jake read the print and sighed, "We have to wait to

use the site until our kit is processed into their database. We might have to wait a couple of hours or up to two days."

"What do we do once it's processed? What'd they do in California?"

Jake folded his arms and stared at the screen. "We check the website for relatives. Once we get one, we'll have to hire a genealogist to walk back that relative's family tree and then explore it out. That's how we get suspects."

Spears did his best to follow along and proudly patted Jake on the shoulder. "You did it, kid. Let me know when it's working."

The captain walked away and left Jake to the website. Jake sat back and stared at the screen admiringly. He felt as though a weight had been lifted off of him. He took comfort in the fact that sometime in the next two days he'd finally have access to what he had set out to do.

Jake showed up to work the next day inspired. He had checked the website repeatedly into the night, but it had still been processing. The excitement made it hard to sleep, and it showed in the morning. His eyes looked sunken, but his spirit was lively. He planned his morning around checking GEDmatch in thirty-minute intervals.

An hour into work and his first two attempts gave him the same result. The database still wasn't available, but on his third try, the website no longer said it was processing his information. He could now use the site. Jake felt a rush of excitement. Who would he find? He knew he might now be a couple of clicks away from discovering a relative to the serial killer he had been investigating from fifty years ago.

Jake called out for Spears over the bullpen and moved his cursor to the "one-to-many" matches link. The captain ran around the cubicles and stood behind Jake. The young detective clicked the link and the website brought him to a new page where he entered the kit number and clicked on "Display results."

A large page opened that resembled a detailed excel table that listed other kit numbers and names. The table appeared complicated, but Jake understood how to read it from the videos he saw online. It was organized with the closest matches filtered to the top. He knew he would navigate the list by a unit of measure called a centimorgan, or cM, a figure that quantifies genetic relationships. Jake had learned that parents shared 3400cM with their child and first cousins would share close to 850cM. He desperately hoped he would find that close of a match.

Spears watched the young detective work the website, speechless. This wasn't a time to be brought up to speed. The captain was more interested in seeing what would happen next. Jake scrolled down through the list of names and aliases. The profiles belonged to real people. He could see that they used Ancestry.com and 23andMe to upload their information. Could one of them be the person they needed? He scrolled back up to the top and started with the first name on the table. Jake followed the row over to a column estimating the number of generations removed that the individual was to the kit he had uploaded, and his heart sank. The closest match wasn't closely related to the Garage Guerrilla at all. The website estimated it was five generations removed. Jake knew this wasn't ideal. Spears could tell that Jake wasn't seeing what he wanted from his body language. He talked to him while Jake stared at the screen. "What do those numbers mean?"

Jake shook his head, unable to break his gaze from the table. He replied, "Hold on."

Jake followed the same row over to the centimorgan column. The match had a number close to 10cM, meaning at best, the individual who owned the account was only a fourth cousin to the Garage Guerrilla. Jake's shoulders dropped. The cM number was too low. There was a chance the person at the top of the list wasn't even related to the Garage Guerrilla. The amount of shared DNA between the two accounts held the same amount of centimorgan shared between individuals of the same race or ancestral origin.

Spears understood by Jake's reaction that the results were not favorable. He asked him again, "What do we got?"

Jake put his head down. He could barely bring himself to say, "We got nothing."

Spears didn't understand. He was looking at a list full of names. He asked, "What do you mean? None of them are actually related?"

Jake didn't lift his head. "Not closely enough."

Everything they had worked on over the weeks had come to nothing. It was a dead-end. Jake got out of his seat and put his hands over his head. Spears sat down on one of the nearby desks and asked, "So, what do we do with this now?"

"Nothing. We can only wait and hope a closer relative volunteers their information."

Spears rubbed the bridge of his nose while he tried to keep his nerve. The news stung. The captain knew this was a potential outcome, but he had let himself become too attached. Not knowing what else to do, Spears got up off of the desk and said, "Keep your head up, kid. What you did here was great detective work. You should be proud of that."

He walked past Jake and headed back to his office. Jake sat down and looked back at the computer screen. If only he was able to use the DNA banks from the larger companies. With their databases, he knew that he would have his relative. GEDmatch was still a comparatively small website. It held over 900,000 DNA kits, but this small number compared to the general population meant there were blind spots in the website's ability to connect people. If the website doubled in size, through genealogy it would be able to identify almost anyone in the United States just from a sample of their DNA.

GEDmatch's largest counterpart is more than twenty times its size. The next-largest DNA collector is more than five times its size. Combined, these companies hold millions of DNA profiles, but they don't offer the services investigators need. They aren't public, and they refuse to work with law enforcement. Jake logged out of the website and put his head in his hands. He had come so close to naming the Garage Guerrilla, but he had come up short. He could only hope GEDmatch would grow in size and that someday, when he logged back on, he'd finally see the match that he was searching for, but only time would tell.

After two weeks, GEDmatch still hadn't produced a closer match to the Garage Guerrilla. Jake worried if people had grown hesitant to sign up after the Golden State Killer case. Yet, in reality, the opposite had occurred. The news had brought the website notoriety and it gained users. Still, the attention wasn't paying off for Jake and Spears.

After they had officially reached the end of their efforts, Chief Kelly quickly rotated Jake under Julie. Jake was now needed in the station's day-to-day matters. Riverwood, like all police departments, suffered from a lack of resources and Jake could no longer be spared. As far as Kelly was concerned the young detective's work on the Garage Guerrilla case had been a success. He had learned valuable lessons and gained considerable experience.

Jake worked on transitioning into the field and helping Julie, but during his lunch hour, he would still find the time to check GEDmatch. He would log in to find the same results and power it down. He knew it could take a long time before he found the match he needed, and he wondered if the Garage Guerrilla was even still alive. The last living officer from the day was the old man, Sean Kennedy. Jake knew he and Spears owed Kennedy a follow-up call. He had told him he'd keep him up to date on the DNA testing but now he felt bad about letting him down.

Jake wasn't sure how to break the news to Kennedy. It would be a hard conversation, but he decided it was better just to get it over with. He mentioned it to Spears and the captain agreed.

On a Friday during their lunch hour, Jake got with Spears to make the call. The young detective took a seat in the captain's office while Spears put the phone on speaker. They listened to the line ring and waited. Jake was nervous to hear how Sean would react to the news. He knew the case meant a lot to him. The line connected and the old man was there. "Mr. Kennedy," Spears began, "it's Captain Alonzo Spears and Detective Jake Caldwell."

Sean was excited to hear from them. His voice gained a pitch. "Captain, how are you doing? It's been a couple of weeks since I've heard from either of you."

"Good, sir. Just calling in to update you."

"I appreciate that. So, what do we got?"

Spears looked over at Jake disappointedly and responded, "Well sir, we checked the DNA against the CODIS system, but unfortunately we didn't get a match." Spears paused briefly and then tried to continue on with a lighter note. "However, we were able to upload the DNA to a different database.

In that, too, we haven't had a match, but It doesn't mean the case is dead. It's more in a stalemate for the moment."

Sean replied, "I'm glad to hear it's still moving."

"Yes, unfortunately, it may take some time, but we figured we owed you the call, sir."

"I sure do appreciate that. I'll be excited to hear from you when you have more. Thanks for the update."

Jake hoped they had a reason to call, too, but he

didn't know if it would ever come. Spears ended the
conversation and hung up the phone. He looked back at
Jake and sighed, "Don't let it get to you. The old man has
had plenty of heartbreak over this case. He can handle
it."

Jake smiled and walked back to the bullpen. He
pulled up GEDmatch one more time, but the website
gave him the same results. Jake sighed. Even though it
hadn't worked for him, he knew that genetic genealogy
would be the future of law enforcement. It had allowed
him to look at a fifty-year-old case with a new chance at
closure. That alone had power. It maybe wouldn't be with
GEDmatch, but someday in the near future investigators
would have the full force of genetic genealogy behind
them. Jake could only wait for that day. He powered
down his computer and left to meet up with Julie.

Chapter 15

2018

It was a Friday night and an old Sean Kennedy was cleaning up the dishes after dinner. He was busy scrubbing away at the mundane task and it made his mind drift. He daydreamed about his grandkids. He thought about baseball games and science fairs, but it didn't last long. It never did. His thoughts always started out well-intentioned but gradually ended up in the same place. His old cases. The ones that got away. It was his mental reset.

It wasn't long after retirement when his wife, Judy, came to know the look. That thousand-yard stare into dead space meant he was somewhere else, reliving a nightmare. She knew that he had retired from a career that he couldn't exactly drop at the door, and she had learned to accept that what her husband had seen, and what he had been through, would always stay with him. In a sense, she felt as though she shared the trauma. He had always been careful not to tell her the worst parts about his career but there were times when he couldn't keep it to himself. The stories Sean told her, affected her in the way that a loved one empathetically imagines pain. She would try to see herself in his shoes, taking the same steps and living through the moment. She had never physically been to a crime scene but through her husband's voice, she had experienced plenty.

Judy watched him finish the dishes. She could see he had the look and she wanted him back. She called out to him, "Sean, you want to watch a movie tonight?"

He turned as if he wasn't expecting to hear someone else's voice but relaxed when he saw his wife and calmly replied, "No. We watched one last night. I was thinking I'd head downstairs tonight."

Judy knew what that meant. The stare had won. A memory from some forgotten injustice was prying at him. Judy understood that she needed to let him see it out. She'd go to the living room and get into her book.

Sean set down the plate he had been drying and headed for the basement. He walked through his living room and stepped over the plush shag carpet they had installed in the 70s. He turned down his hallway and headed for the stairs. Floorboards creaked behind him and followed his footsteps. He made his way down the stairs and found his study. There Sean flicked on the light and stared at old file boxes piled to the ceiling. They contained the cases Sean couldn't let go of, homicides that he never found the answers to. A few cases kept his interest over the years but most of the boxes were full of files from just one. The Garage Guerrilla.

Kennedy walked over to his desk where he had one of the boxes singled out from the others. He opened the box and pulled out a file from 1969. He started to read over the Janet Oliver homicide, but at the first words, his inspiration began to fade. He had already forgotten the thought that pulled him into the basement. Frustrated, he rubbed his eyes. Sean had read the same pages so many times that they all seemed to blend together into one big mess. He tried to recall the memory that brought him to his study, but it had escaped him. He knew it would find him again when he least expected it — during another round of dishes or, more likely, in the middle of a sleepless night.

He stared at the wall in front of him and wondered if he was wasting his time. He thought about his friends who played golf, chess and poker. Games they focused their lives around and always produced a different outcome. They gave his friends something to think about, something to do, but Sean couldn't do them. Every time someone mentioned he needed to enjoy his golden years more, he would get mad. He still had something to do, something to think about. Something that wasn't finished.

In the last couple of years, he had tried his best to

focus on new hobbies. His wife urged him to spend his time doing anything else besides his old work. She couldn't stand seeing him torture himself over the past. But ever since he had received a call from the Riverwood Police about his most obsessive case, the files had won him back. He couldn't stop himself from diving into it once again. Even after all these years, he still carried a sense of optimism that he would see something he'd missed before. The hope was always short-lived, but it was frequent enough to keep him checking the files at least once a week.

As of late, Sean had been slipping into his study more often, but the case was making him more frustrated than it had before. His quick temper came from the angst he had built up in waiting for another call from the Riverwood captain and detective who had reached out to him before. To Sean, it sounded like they were making progress with the DNA, but he didn't know how much, or how significant it would be in finally closing the case. His last call with the Riverwood team had been four months ago and he was beginning to wonder if he'd ever hear from them again.

Sean decided he had been in the dark long enough. He needed to speak with the Riverwood police. He pulled out an old brick of a cell phone from one of the drawers in his desk. He rarely used the old phone, mainly when he left home for long periods — that was, if he even remembered it. But it came in handy time and again when he needed to have a private conversation. One that Judy couldn't listen to if she picked up the other line in the living room.

The cell phone was practically an antique. Bought in the late 2000s, it would soon be ten years old. Kennedy powered it on and found where he had written down the Riverwood station number. When he called, the phone sounded fuzzy. The reception wasn't good in his basement. The line connected and a woman answered the phone. "Riverwood police, what can I do for you?"

Sean looked over at another scrap piece of paper where he had written down names. He spoke as he read it. "Hello, I'm retired Captain Sean Kennedy. I'm calling for Captain Spears."

The woman responded, "I'm sorry, Captain Spears isn't in today. Would you like to leave a message?"

Kennedy looked back over at the scrap of paper. "Is Detective Caldwell available?"

"Yes, he is. I'll transfer you over."

Sean thanked her and stayed on the line. Moments later, Jake answered the phone. "Mr. Kennedy. Good evening, sir. How are you?"

He was happy to hear Jake's voice. He smiled as he responded, "I'm good, detective. I've been alright."

Jake immediately understood why the old man was calling. Knowing where Kennedy would take the call, he got ahead of the conversation and said, "I'm sorry I haven't gotten back to you. They've moved me out into the field, and I've been busy with other things. Time's been flying by."

Sean knew there could only be two reasons why Jake and his captain hadn't called. Either they had moved away from the case or they had bad news they didn't want to break him. He hoped they had only gotten busy. Sean was fully aware that cold cases couldn't afford all the attention. It was difficult for a police unit to move resources away from the incoming workload they had. He could sense where the conversation was going by Jake's response, but he pressed on anyway and said, "That's ok, detective. I know how it is. I just figured I'd give you a ring and see if you'd had any news?"

Jake replied, "Well sir, I've been checking on the case at least every other day but unfortunately our status is still the same. We still don't have a viable match."

The news was disappointing to Sean, but he held onto the hope that they had given him from their last call. He asked, "Is there still a chance?"

"Yes, sir. There definitely is. The big question is just when it's going to come."

Sean felt reassured. He had heard the update he'd called in for and didn't want to waste any more of Jake's time. He replied, "Well, I appreciate the news, detective. Just figured I'd bug you."

Jake sympathized with the old man. "I'm sorry I don't have more for you, sir," he replied. "I'll keep checking on it. Feel free to call back anytime. I'll give you my cell number so you can reach me directly. If I get anything, you're my first call."

Sean respected the gesture. He took Jake's number and put it in his cellphone. After that, he ended the conversation. Sean put his phone down and looked at the old paperwork lying in front of him. It looked like a nightmare, a never-ending story he couldn't get away from. He decided he had done enough with it for the night. He'd call it early and take his wife up on that movie.

Dissatisfied, he slowly put the paperwork away. He stacked the files back in the box on his desk and put the lid over it. He knew he'd be back soon.

It was an average Thursday night at the Kennedy household and the old man couldn't finish his dinner. Almost a week had passed since Sean rung up Jake at the station. He had tried to think less about the case after that call, but an idea came to him that gave him the urge to venture downstairs. It was always the faint grasp of a memory that got him. The idea that something left behind from fifty-year-old notes might suddenly bring him to a new realization.

He looked up from his now cold potatoes, across the table to Judy and told her, "I think I'm going down to the study tonight."

"Ok. I can take care of the dishes."

He smiled at his wife and got up from the table. He quickly made it down to his study, hoping to beat the idea from leaving him. The room looked just as he had left it the week before. The box he had been looking over was still on his desk. Sean walked over to it and sat down. He reached out to put his hand on the lid but remembered the discouraging Déjà-vu the files inside gave him. Maybe he'd go for a different box tonight, one he had been neglecting for a while. Perhaps that was where the note he needed lived.

He walked over to his wall of boxes and picked one covered in dust. Sean worked it out of the stack and brought it over to his desk. He pulled the lid off and exposed the bundles of files filled with yellowed paper. He pulled one out and scanned it over. He instantly recognized its pages. The same feeling of discouraging Déjà-vu came over him. It was a hopeless feeling knowing he had already read every word on the pages in front of him. If they couldn't help him before, what could they do now? He tried to remember if there was anything interesting to look at, but nothing came to mind. The discouragement festered into frustration. It was the same frustration that had kept him out of the basement for the last week.

Sean felt cursed. He'd woken up so many nights over the case and just wanted to be at ease. He looked back at the box with a lack of motivation. Was this how he wanted to spend another night? Would it be another waste? He felt his anger building and decided it wasn't worth his time. He slammed the lid on the file box and marched upstairs. There he found Judy working on the dishes. She was surprised to see him and said, "That was fast."

"I couldn't do it tonight. It's all just messing with my head."

Judy nodded and calmly responded, "Well, do you want to go out for a walk?"

Sean shook his head. "No. Not tonight. I like the idea of getting out to clear my head, but to be honest, I want to go get a beer. Do you want to get a drink?"

Judy laughed. Her husband rarely drank, and she wasn't much of a drinker either. She couldn't even remember the last time they had gone out for a drink. She replied, "No. I think I'll stay home and relax."

She assumed that if she wouldn't go, he'd change his mind and stay back with her, but Sean was determined. He replied, "Ok. I think I'm just going to go get a beer. I need a change of scenery."

"Do you want a ride?"

Sean waved her off. "No, I'll drive."

He headed for the door, but Judy called after him,

"At least take your cell phone. That way I can get ahold of you if I think of anything we need from the store while you're out."

Sean sighed and turned back for his phone. He hurried down to his study and grabbed it before he left.

It was around 7 p.m. when Sean pulled up to an old red-bricked bar sitting off of a strip of new shops and restaurants. The area had gone through a lot of changes over the years, but the bar made it through. He parked his car and headed inside. The bar itself hadn't changed since the last time he'd been there. It still had the smell of cheap beer and pizza. The room was dimly lit and held a collage of neon signs on its back wall. A pool table sat in the center where two younger guys were playing and drinking pints. If it wasn't for the sight of an occasional cell phone the bar could've passed as a scene from two decades before.

Sean walked over and grabbed a stool at the bar. He looked up and down the row. Besides the two guys playing pool there were only a couple of other people scattered about. Sean saw an old man swaying in the back corner by the dartboard and squinted at him to see him better. The man was around his age and piss drunk. He turned to look at the others but was interrupted by the bartender.

"What can I get you?"

He looked past the bartender and tried to recognize any of the taps behind him. He couldn't make out one and kept his order simple by saying, "I'll take a pilsner."

The bartender nodded and walked away. Sean couldn't help but notice the music being played from the jukebox. It was annoyingly loud rock that came from the overhead speakers. He recognized it as 80s hair metal, which wasn't his favorite.

The bartender returned with his drink and he paid him in cash. Sean grabbed the beer in front of him and held it admiringly. It was gold in color, condensation already appearing on the outside of the glass. He lifted it up and took a long drink. The flavor was a throwback to his younger years. He set the glass down and let himself relax. This was what he wanted. A different setting than his basement or living room. There were people to listen to and drama to absorb. It was the same reason he had loved going to the Ralston Cafe all those years ago. Sean didn't like talking to strangers but for some reason, he enjoyed having them around. Hearing them bicker about their day was oddly calming for him. It made him feel like he wasn't the only one. He took comfort in the fact that other people were just as upset about their struggles as he was with his. It made him feel normal.

He took another sip of his beer and tried to tune out the hair band music. He focused on the feel of the cold glass in his hand. He turned to watch the younger guys play pool when someone loudly sat next to him at the bar. He looked over and saw another older man. The stranger didn't seem to notice that he had just taken the seat next to Sean when nearly every other seat in the bar was available. The man turned to him and smiled to say, "Good to see another old-timer tearing up the place."

Sean politely smiled back and turned away, annoyed. He had no intention of talking to anyone besides the bartender and he definitely didn't want to sit elbow-to-elbow with another guy when they had the whole bar. The stranger stuck out his hand and started to introduce himself.

"Name's Don Williams."

Sean sighed. He didn't want to face him. The stranger was killing his mood. He could have stayed home with Judy and taken her up on that walk, but now he had to talk to some guy named Don and listen to Def Leppard. In an attempt at civility, Sean turned back around and took Don's hand. He kept his hello short and only said, "Sean." At first, he looked the stranger in the eye until his old habit kicked in and he glanced down at his hand. He briefly looked at it and began to look up at the man's face, but his gaze shot back to the hand. It had a scar. *The* scar. In between the thumb and index finger on his right hand. It crept all the way up to his wrist.

Don noticed that Sean was staring at his scar and broke the awkward silence over it.

"Oh, that. That's what carving a turkey does for you after a bottle of whiskey." Don laughed. "Put the knife right in my hand."

Sean looked up at him with a dull expression. He had shaken so many scarred hands over the years, but he had never seen this one. After fifty years of suspecting everyone with a right-handed scar, the situation seemed almost funny. Sean thought to himself that of course, this would happen to him tonight. He looked into the man's eyes and thought, *No way. Not now. Not tonight when I just wanted a break from the whole thing.*

Sean nodded at Don's story, unsure and unmotivated to take the conversation anywhere else. Don ordered a beer and started talking again. He said, "Are you a regular here?"

Sean let out another sigh. He couldn't believe this was the night he had left his house for. He began to regret the whole thing. He knew that he couldn't get out of the conversation. Don had made it plenty clear that no matter how uninterested Sean looked, they were going to talk. Sean made his peace with the moment and responded to Don, "No, I'm not a regular here. I just wanted a beer."

Don took the reply as an invitation to tell his own story. He replied, "Yeah, me too. I used to live around here but moved away. My brother is still out here so I see him from time to time." Don continued talking but Sean tuned him out. He had retreated into his own thoughts and pushed Don out with the same mental block as the hair band music. He watched the man as he blabbered on with his story and glanced back down to his hand. The cut looked like it had been deep. The scar tissue was once bubbled and pronounced. The guy himself said it had come from a kitchen knife. Sean's mental reset was kicking in and he tried not to put himself back in the cold case headspace, but he couldn't help it. This man had literally sat down in front of him.

Don noticed that Sean was tuning him out and spoke up.

"So anyway, that's how I found this place."

Sean looked up from his hand and back at him. He nodded to try and convince Don he had been listening to him the whole time. Don pointed at Sean's beer and asked, "Are you getting another round?"

Sean looked over at his now empty beer. He hadn't even noticed that he had finished it. He was staring too hard at Don's hand. He looked back over at him and replied, "Sure."

The bartender came over and poured them another round. Sean started to pull out his wallet, but Don stopped him by saying, "No it's fine. I got a tab going on my card. I got yours."

Sean smiled and put his wallet back while replying, "Ok. Thanks, Don."

All he had planned on doing was drinking one beer, but he knew he couldn't walk away from that scar. Sean looked Don up and down while he talked to the bartender. He noticed that Don had thin greying hair that used to be black. He was around 5'10" and had a build that suggested at one time he could have been athletic. The vague profile fit. He appeared to be the right age, but If Sean was being serious with himself and was honestly thinking suspiciously of this new stranger, how would he go about it? How could he sit there and prove that it was him? How could he not embarrass himself as he had time and time before with every guy who was unlucky enough to have a similar scar?

Sean realized he didn't care if he made a fool out of himself and that's when the idea came to him. He needed Don's DNA. The new detective, Jake, had told him on the phone that they had already identified the Garage Guerrilla's DNA, but they were still waiting on a match. Kennedy leaned into his habit of suspicion and began to believe there was a chance he was sitting next to it, but how could he pull it off? He thought to himself, *Maybe I can get his hair.* He looked at the thinning hair on the man's head. It would have to be on his clothes. He squinted down at his coat and tried to see if he could spot any. He thought for a brief second about stealing the coat but reasoned it off as causing too much of a scene. He brought his eyes back up to Don's as the man went into his next story. Maybe he could wipe his mouth or his face with a napkin?

Kennedy stared hard into Don, looking to the other man as though he was interested in the one-sided conversation. Don continued to ramble on, happy to have an ear to preach to. Kennedy took breaks from the noise by drinking his beer. As he put down a large gulp another idea hit him. It was perfect. Kennedy said to himself, internally, *I need his glass.*

He looked over at Don, who was still talking. He focused his eyes on Don's beer. It was close to empty. He looked back at his own glass and noticed that it was almost finished as well. The alcohol's effects were beginning to hit him. His age and lack of drinking made the two beers do a number on him. Sitting in the chair and listening to Don was becoming easier. Don spoke up again to get Sean's attention and asked, "You getting another round?"

Sean looked over at him and shook his head. "No. You?"

He didn't want another beer but if Don stayed, he had no choice but to stick it out. Luckily Don also shook his head and replied, "No, if you're leaving, I'll probably head out too."

Sean was happy to hear it, but now he realized he

had to somehow get the glass and fast. If the bartender came too early and took it what would he do? They still had enough beers in their glasses to give him a little time. Don waved the bartender down and asked him for the bill. Sean watched him sign for the beers and put his credit card back in his wallet. Don turned back to Sean when he was done signing and said, "Well, good talking to you."

"Yeah. You too."

Sean waved his hand as a goodbye gesture and Don got up from his seat. He finished his beer and shook Sean's hand one more time. Sean watched him leave and turned back to the glass. The bartender was coming to pick it up. He had to beat him to it. Sean knew that if he didn't grab the glass, he'd never let himself forget it. The bartender reached for the empty glass, but Sean put his hand on it first. The bartender stared at him confused and asked, "Are you done with that?"

Sean didn't know how to explain why he needed Don's empty glass; all he could think of was. "Not yet."

The bartender decided not to waste his time with it and walked away. Sean slid his almost finished beer over and now only held Don's. He knew that what he had just done with the glass was strange, but he didn't care. Now he needed to plan how he was going to leave with it.

He slowly got up from the bar and walked over near

the young guys playing pool. He pretended to be interested in their game as he made his way around the table. The bartender was watching him out of curiosity but became occupied with another customer. Sean kept walking around the pool table until he was close to the door. He looked around the bar to see if anyone was watching him and then walked outside.

Sean stepped out into an autumn evening excited and a little buzzed. He laughed to himself. *Did I really just do that? What the hell am I going to do with this thing now?* He walked over to his car and got in. He set the glass in his cup holder and stared at it. He thought about driving it down to the station and trying to drop it off at the front desk when he remembered that his wife had made him take his cell phone.

Sean pulled it out of his pocket and turned it on. The green screen came to life. He had put Jake's cell number in his contacts. He opened the phone book and found the detective's name. Sean hit the call button and put the phone to his ear.

The phone rang twice, and Sean tapped his hand on his lap. "Come on, come on." The line connected and Jake answered the phone, "Hello?"

Sean felt a rush of relief that he hadn't put the wrong number in. He wasn't sure how he was going to explain the situation and started talking before he figured it out. He replied, "Detective, it's Sean Kennedy."

Jake was confused to be hearing from the man so late and said, "Mr. Kennedy, what can I do for you?"

Sean struggled to explain himself. "Um, well. I hope I got you at a good time?"

"Is everything alright?"

Sean found his explanation and got to the point. "Yes, everything's fine, but you're not going to believe this. I have something that you need to test at the lab."

Jake didn't know how to respond. The comment caught him off guard. He eventually said, "I'm sorry, what, sir?"

"I have something that you need to test at the lab."

Jake thought that was what he said. He replied, "Did you find something in your files?"

"No. This is something new. Remember what I told you about the scar?"

"The scar that should be on the Garage Guerrilla's hand?"

The old man confirmed. "Yes, exactly. Well, I met a guy tonight. A guy who had that exact scar."

Jake wasn't sure what to think. He began to feel bad for the old man. He knew that he couldn't let the case go but he didn't know it was this bad. He wondered if he shouldn't have given him his cell number. Sean came back over the line, "Jake, he matched the description perfectly. He had the scar; it came from a knife. He told me that himself."

Jake still wasn't convinced. "Mr. Kennedy, are you sure about this?"

"Detective. I wouldn't be calling you if I wasn't."

Jake decided to take the old man for his word and believed him. He asked, "What is it that you have and where'd you meet this guy?"

"I'm at a bar on Colfax Avenue. I took his beer glass. Jake, I know this sounds odd, but you have to believe me."

Jake was worried that Kennedy was drunk, but he was now interested in the glass. If the old man was telling the truth, then it was beyond happenstance. He replied, "Mr. Kennedy, are you alright to drive?"

"Yeah, yeah."

Jake thought of where they could meet and responded, "Ok Mr. Kennedy, if you're on Colfax, then the station is in between us. I can meet you in the parking lot in 20 minutes."

"Ok. I'll see you there."

When Jake pulled his car into the station's parking lot, Sean Kennedy was already there. He was standing outside of his car, smoking a cigarette. He put it out when Jake parked next to him. Jake got out of his car and called out to the old man, "You got it?"

Sean opened his front door and pulled out a pint

glass from his cup holder. He held it out for Jake and replied, "I know this sounds crazy but what do we have to lose?"

Jake looked at him and could see how serious Sean was. He leaned into his car and pulled out a pair of gloves and a small wine box filled with newspaper. He put the gloves on and walked over to look at the glass. Sean handed it to him carefully and said, "I didn't touch the edges and I only held the bottom. His lips and his hands were all over this thing." Jake took the glass and Sean explained himself again. "Detective, I know this seems stupid. You just got to do this for me."

Jake nodded. He would give it to the lab. He could see how sincere the old man was. Any doubts that he had over the phone he now looked beyond strictly out of respect for the man. He put the glass in the wine box and closed the lid. Jake looked back up at Sean, he said, "I believe you. Working on this case as long as you have, this is the least I can do."

Sean nodded and thanked him. Jake walked back over to his car and spoke to him before he got in. "I'll drop this off at the lab tomorrow morning. I'll let you know what we hear, it shouldn't take long. Get home. It's cold out here."

Jake got in his car and waved goodbye to Sean. The old man smiled and pulled out another cigarette. He was cold but he wanted to relish the moment. He was glad that he had the guts to fight off the embarrassment of stealing the glass. He couldn't help feeling a bit like a fool, but he knew that if he didn't go through with it, he would have never let himself forget it. He watched Jake drive away and enjoyed his cigarette, happier than he had been in a long time. He knew that for once, he'd be able to sleep for a night.

The next morning Sean woke up early. He made a pot of coffee and sat on the couch to watch the news. He had slept soundly through the night, but now that he was up the morning painted his evening in a different perspective. He couldn't stop the feeling that he had made an embarrassment of himself. He kept shaking his head and tried to recall exactly how the night went. He tried hard to bring back the mental image of Don's hand, but the memory was already fading from the amount of pressure he was putting on himself. He thought about calling Jake to apologize but talked himself out of it. He knew he needed to get his mind off of it and he figured he'd save his apology for when Jake called him to tell him the glass didn't match what they had at the lab.

Sean nervously devoted his day to chores and tried to busy himself with them. He did his best to think beyond the day and planned out his weekend with Judy. When she asked about his night, he kept his answers brief and changed the subject. The day began to move along, and Sean went about it as he planned.

In the afternoon, he found himself cleaning the garage and organizing his tools when the phone rang in the house. His stomach churned but he let Judy pick it up and acted as if he wasn't expecting a call. Sean tried to focus back on the task at hand, but he couldn't help from listening to his wife's muffled voice through the walls. Maybe the call wasn't for him. He got back into cleaning the garage, but he heard Judy walking for the door. The call was for him. His stomach churned again. The embarrassment would be overwhelming. What was he going to say to Jake? He decided it was better if he just accepted that he had acted foolishly and was honest with the young detective.

Judy opened the garage door and looked over at her husband. "Sean, honey, phone." He walked over and grabbed the phone from his wife. When he put it to his ear it was Jake.

"Mr. Kennedy, how are you feeling today?"

Jake's voice was a little higher pitched than usual. Sean swallowed his pride and began to apologize. He replied, "Jake, I just want to say I'm sorry. I had a couple of drinks and I embarrassed myself."

Jake tried to cut him off. "Mr. Kennedy–"

"I don't drink that often," Sean continued, "and I've been thinking about the case a lot lately."

Jake tried to stop him again. "Mr. Kennedy—"

Sean continued talking, "I don't know where my head was at, but I can't stress enough how embarrassed I am and how sorry I am that I wasted your time."

Jake yelled at him over the phone, "Sean!"

The old man finally stopped talking and let Jake get a word in. Jake waited until he was sure Sean wasn't going to say anything else and replied, "It matched."

The words didn't register at first. Moments ago, Sean couldn't stop talking, but now he had nothing to say. Jake told him again, "It *matched,* sir. Whose ever lips touched that glass you gave me last night also happened to have left their blood behind at the Kathrine Sandoval and Janet Oliver murders."

Sean was rendered speechless. He grabbed to hold onto something. From his silence, the young detective asked for him, "Did you hear me, Mr. Kennedy?"

Sean's voice was shaky but finally came over the phone. "Are you sure?"

"We're 99% certain."

Sean struggled to reply. After all of the years he had put into the case, this was the moment he had been waiting for, but now that it was here, he wasn't sure what to do with himself. He wanted to laugh and cry at the same time. Jake stole his attention back and said, "However, there is one issue and we're hoping it's something you can help us with. We have the man's DNA, but we don't have his name. Do you know how we can find the guy?"

Sean's emotions blended together and overwhelmed him. With tears in his eyes, he replied, "He paid with a card."

Afterword

The novel you've just read was inspired by a true story. During the late 60s and 70s, in the neighborhoods west of Denver, there was a prowler known as the Garage Guerrilla (Gorilla). Just as in the story, the real Garage Gorilla cowardly preyed on women by waiting for them in their garages and later by turning on their garden hoses.

Never known to have actually committed a murder, the Garage Gorilla gained infamy and spread terror after multiple sexual assaults. The community amplified the man's story, and tales of a night stalker roaming the streets spread throughout Denver's suburbs.

It's through these passed down stories that I came to know the name. My father, who was a child at the time, had a similar experience to the young boy, Michael Martin, whose story I tell in Chapter 11. A haunting thought for me to recall, since it meant the real predator once targeted my family. No arrest was ever made in the case, and if the real Garage Gorilla is still alive, then he most likely remains in the community that he terrorized all those years ago.

Even though this was a fictionalized story its foundations were from very real places and cases. As I write these words the Golden State Killer is still awaiting trial in Sacramento. Although he has not yet been tried, the Seattle case mentioned in chapter 12 was the first to use genetic genealogy and GEDmatch to go to trial and successfully reach a guilty verdict, locking in the Golden State Killer's fate and acknowledging the legality of the investigation's methods.

All three of the cases that inspired this story were crimes involving sexual assault and all three of these cases are examples of real offenders who successfully timed out their statute of limitations on sexual assault. After the Golden State Killer was identified and arrested, the Sacramento district attorney was unable to bring one charge of rape against him by law. A man who committed over 50 rapes wasn't charged for one.

As of 2020, 43 states still have a statute of limitations on sexual assault and rape, allowing offenders the ability to wait out their rightful sentence.

In the wake of the Golden State Killer case, GEDmatch was thrust onto the public stage. In May of 2018, GEDmatch changed its terms of service and website to allow the transparent use of its database for law enforcement and its private sector affiliates. It even added a link for investigators to use directly on its homepage. The website quickly gained notability and went on to assist investigators in tens of other cold cases. The ancestry website was at the forefront of a new era in law enforcement until it came under fire for being used to name a young man who carried out an aggravated assault on an elderly woman. Due to the fact that the woman was not sexually assaulted and survived the attack, some called foul.

Critics of the police action claimed that investigators had gone too far on a case that didn't deserve the attention. They reasoned that police authority was on a slippery slope to exploiting the privacy of the greater population through the use of a public website. Their main argument, being that as people signed up to use GEDmatch, they did it in the hopes of finding distant relatives and not for the unknown use of law enforcement.

GEDmatch agreed with the critics and in May of 2019 rewrote its terms of service, but more importantly, added a disclaimer to its users. The disclaimer allowed users to opt into ongoing police investigations. If a person didn't actively opt-in to assist law enforcement their account was automatically opted out, effectively shutting down the machine that solved so many cold cases.

By the time this action was taken, GEDmatch had grown to over one million users. All were removed as an investigative resource overnight, closing the door on the monumental progress GEDmatch had paved the way for.

In a world where every website you browse, every app you use and every purchase you make is all knowingly tracked in the interest of exploiting your choices for the sole gain of private interests, the use of a public website to apprehend the nation's criminals seems justified. However, the fear of bureaucracy profiting from the sale or exploitation of a national DNA database is also justified. The debate surrounding this issue is just as complicated as any, but the gains in justice seem too good to ignore.

If you had to make the choice between solving homicides or protecting the population's DNA privacy, what would you choose? Could you knowingly deny the redemption to hundreds of new and old criminal cases?

There isn't an easy answer, because there isn't a clear outcome. But no matter how the future unfolds, people will ultimately have to make the choice between unmasking killers or maintaining the perception of their dwindling privacy.

Acknowledgements

Thanks to all the friends and family who helped me along the way. Especially Kia Fritz, who had to listen to all of my enthusiasm and ideas, and whose motivation kept me going. Thanks to my editor, book designer and cover artist, whose contributions brought the book together. A special thanks to Nick Pirog for lending an ear and pointing me in the right direction.

CPSIA information can be obtained
at www.ICGtesting.com
Printed in the USA
FSHW010817190121
77793FS